Just the Guys

Arian Mabe

This is a collection of short stories focusing on gay furry erotica.

This story collection covers: male characters only, gay erotica, furry characters, human furries at a convention, fursuit sex, transformation, oral sex, anal sex, rimming, public & semi-public sex, BDSM, domination/submission play, bondage, first time sex and romance.

Trigger warning: Strangers in Vegas contains a mention of coerced sex in the context of trauma. The sexual scene in the story is fully consensual.

Table of Contents

Beach Days

Kevin grinned, peering at his wolf partner down by the water, the heat of summer licking at his red fur. It was good to bare it all – or, nearly all – at the beach at last, for neither the fox nor the wolf lived near the coast usually. A weekend away, to get away from the grind of work and general life drudgery, was exactly what the doctor ordered for the two of them.

He groaned softly, a pink flick of tongue snaking out against the side of his muzzle. Charlie, or Charles, if his more formal name was ever used, splashed about in the shallows with the joy of a wolf cub, kicking and spinning in the dying rays of the day. The sunset cast red and orange shades over his grey fur, hiding that Charlie had dyed red streaks into his fur, which added an extra dimension to his natural colouration.

It was good to see Char being so relaxed out there, for the wolf was often so tightly strung and tense that Kevin just didn't know how he kept it together for so long. But that was where the fox came into play there, as he felt better placed to help out his partner and make sure he took the time off he needed simply to rest and recharge. Kevin ran a more relaxed kind of life, working from home and not bustling through a hectic commute on the roads every day like Charlie did, although they fit together. Could they really have ever asked for anything more than that?

It was enough for them to be themselves, for them to be together just as they needed to be. Sometimes couples didn't match up perfectly, odds and ends sticking out at funny angles, but Kevin was simply grateful to be able to do one little thing for Char in taking him out for a weekend away, all to take a break.

"Hey, Kevin!"

The wolf waved, grinning and holding something high above his head. Kevin suppressed a shudder and smiled back at him, though he thought Char was rather a lot braver than he was, considering the crab he was holding up was still waving its little claws around. He wasn't so good with scratchy, scrabbly things, though he appreciated his boyfriend's vivacious nature. Nothing seemed to set him back.

And, frankly, Kevin never wanted to see Charlie at the point where he couldn't handle things anymore, where he went over the edge. Anything he could do to keep things right in his partner's life was simply automatic for him.

"It looks cool, sweetie!" Kevin called back, half-cupping a paw to his muzzle as his short, fox-ish whiskers tickled his paw. "Why don't you come over here?"

The beach they'd chosen was rocky with towering cliffs behind; as it was on the West side of the country, they were able to watch the sun setting over the sea. It had been a long climb down the tight, winding steps hewn into the side of the cliff, glad of the safety rail, but it had been worth it in the end. It was secluded and they'd only seen a few other couples there the whole day long, the rasp of waves rolling to the shore soothing to the twitch of his ears.

The sight of his partner bounding up to him, the crab set safely into a rock pool, made his heart leap and, in his swim trunks, his sheath tingled faintly. Why did it take so little for him to get aroused? The fox licked his lips, hiding his smirk, his dark glasses pushed a little further down his muzzle, the clips on the sides of the arms irritating his fur. Kevin was glad he didn't have to wear glasses full time, for it was not the most comfortable thing for him personally.

Yet Char rippled with moderate muscle, his body lean like that of a swimmer. He worked out some but not enough to really build muscle, considering how active he was daily. Charlie simply didn't eat enough and that would always restrict how he developed muscle physically. Kevin, on the other paw, had enough time to work out in the local gym, which was good enough for him, even if it was not like the rough industrial gym he'd joined back in his early twenties. The fox had many good memories of that place, but he'd moved on from it, as was the way of life.

Still, he would have gone back if he'd had the chance, all so he could enjoy the eye candy and get a good sweat on. He was still more muscular than Char as a result of his extra time to work out and it seemed that the wolf was set to take full advantage of that as he flopped on to the fox's chest with a heavy thump.

"Oof!" Kevin grunted, his red tail swishing off to the side, though it didn't need to make room for his boyfriend. "Hey, watch it, you're going to hit things you don't wanna there."

Even then, Kevin couldn't keep the flirt out of his tone, smirking faintly as his lips quirked up a little more on the side. Charlie squirmed on top of him and the fox was grateful, at least, that he was on a towel spread out on the sand. If he'd been on a sun lounger, which they'd left up in the car in the grassy car park on top of the cliff, it may well have not taken both of their weights together.

As it was, he was free to wrap his arms around the wolf and hug him tightly, burying his snout into the rough fur of his neck. On top of him, Charlie let out soft grunts and groans, lips stretching into an easy grin, the tension having slipped from his shoulders. The fox smiled, inhaling his scent, which was tinged with salt after the day at the beach, though there was male musk under it and the spicy aroma of Char's fur wash mixed in there too.

"Mmmm…" Charlie groaned, nuzzling back and stealing a kiss to the side of the fox's lips. "Thanks for bringing me here, babe, this was just what I needed."

Kevin grinned.

"I think I always know what you need," he said, his voice softening with affection. "It's just getting you to accept it and take the time that's a little bit of a problem here."

"I know, I know," Char whined, but accepted the admonishment. "But it's good, if I'm with you… You know? Does that make sense?"

Kevin laughed. The wolf hadn't said very much at all and yet the fox understood him perfectly.

Oh, you…

"Yeah, of course, babe," he said easily. "I'd do anything for you."

Char sat up, sitting astride Kevin's hips with a glint in his eye. The wolf was anything but subtle.

"Mmm… Well, I wouldn't mind seeing a bit of that," Char said, a little seductive as he rolled his crotch down against Kevin's crotch. "You know… There's no one else around…"

"Oh…"

Kevin groaned, the fox thrusting up softly against his partner, following the lead of their bodies coming together. Sand clung to the fur of his hind paw, digging in around the heel, though Kevin didn't pay it all that much mind. There were better things to consider, like the bulge rising through the front of Char's loose shorts. Even if they weren't ones designed for being worn in the water, they were damp from his time splashing about in the ocean, the sun dipping lower towards the horizon.

"Mm, aren't you worried about someone seeing?" Kevin teased, palming that bulge and cupping his fingers around it. "It's still a public beach, you know."

Charlie whined and shook his head. The fox didn't have the tuft of thicker hair-like fur on the top of his head that Char did and he'd always admired the shade of purple there. It was eye-catching, hardly a shade that would naturally be found with wolves, though Kevin had heard Charlie was sick of comments on it. The hair wasn't all that professional, technically, for a more traditional workplace, although he wasn't willing to dye it to something more neutral either.

It was funny those little concessions anthros made when they had to work – which was the case for most in the world, of course. But no one should ever have had to change how they were naturally just to "fit in."

"Mmm, I'm not worried, it's late enough," Charlie breathed, tipping forward over Kevin's body to brush their muzzles tenderly together. "Besides… Don't you want me to take care of this?"

He took the chance to rub his paw over Kevin's rising hard-on, though his cock was still only halfway out of his sheath and partly soft. It made an obvious bulge, however, in his swim trunks, the fabric thankfully dry after he'd taken a little dip in the water earlier. Even though it was a good look seeing swim trunks or shorts clinging to a rising, hard bulge, it was not the most comfortable sensation for him, at the very least.

But it was enough for him to roll his hips sensually up against Charlie's paw as he ground into it. His need rose as he licked his lips, swiping his pink tongue down the side of his muzzle in a long, lewd lap.

"Mmm… I do, if you're brave enough to take the leap," Kevin said at last, though it was hard to talk while he was more focused on his cock swelling, over three-quarters of it protruding from his sheath. "But I didn't think you'd ever be so forward about it. I *love* it."

Charlie blushed and whined, squirming a little on top of him – though the time was right for him to take charge and roll the two of them over on to the towel next to his. A little sand spilled on to it, following the creases in the absorbent material, but neither the fox nor the wolf paid much mind to it. A little sand in their fur was just a side effect of heading down to the beach, even if neither had expected that kind of fun.

"Mm, you look so much better on the bottom, darling," Kevin growled, pinning Charlie down lightly by his shoulders. "But I think you're going to blow before me this time."

He nuzzled into the wolf's neck as he worked his way down Char's body. Kevin's tail swung with single-minded intent as he growled playfully, his heart beating harder than normal. Time was of the essence, the beach and surrounding land, even up on the cliffs, seemingly deserted. But anyone could come by, perhaps someone who knew a gentler way down to the sands for an evening walk, forcing them to move swiftly.

The fox's skin prickled deliciously, however, with the threat of getting caught. Why was that so alluring? He'd fucked around in lifts and in the car with a couple of previous boyfriends, before Charlie, but it wasn't really something he'd dug into all that much. Yet the rising throb of need coursed through his cock divinely, pumping it up firmly as the tip pressed into his shorts.

He let it be for the moment, however, rolling his hips a little in a thrust as he peeled down Char's shorts. His trunks highlighted the shape of his body and the extra softness around his rump, though Kevin was glad merely to see the hard spring of his cock once it was fully freed from his clothes and sheath.

"Ah, there it is…" He breathed, sparing Charlie a wink as the wolf whined and lay back, an arm half cast across his face. "And to think you were keeping this hidden from me. Were you thinking about me while you were out there in the water?"

"Mmph… How do you always know?"

Char squirmed under him as if he simply could not stay still, his tail trying to wag where it was half pinned under his rump. But the wolf obliged him by staying as still as he could while Kevin took his liberties with his body, focusing on his cock. He spared the wolf's balls a slight squeeze, enjoying their comfortable weight in the palm of his paw, but slid his paw up quickly to the treat of his cock.

The skin of Charlie's sheath pulled along with his paw for a moment before his palm and fingers glided along smooth flesh. A bead of slickness at the tip, however faint, betrayed the wolf's arousal and Kevin smirked, licking his lips again. It was a little reflex, but he wasn't all that willing to think about his own actions all that much when he had his partner there to adore.

The little moans and whimpers rising from the wolf's lips were delicious, though not as much as his cock. The fox took the hard length seductively between his lips as he slid his head down, using his lips as a tight seal around the girth. The tapered tip was thicker than his own, although comparing sizes had never been all that much of a concern between them.

"Mmph, ah… Your muzzle…" Charlie groaned, struggling to get words out. "It feels… Mm!"

The wolf didn't have to get words out, however, for Kevin to understand what he wanted and all he craved. It was coming, the wolf's orgasm, yet the fox was more than willing to draw it out for as long as he sensibly could, considering the situation.

He rumbled a soft, testing growl around his partner's cock, letting the subtle vibrations travel into

Charlie's crotch for an added touch of sensation. Sucking the wolf's cock was one thing, but he wanted to do even more than that, leaning into the moment as his ears splayed out softly to the sides of his head.

It was easier, just like that, to slip into the moment and forget the rest of the world. Some would have caused it submission, but Kevin simply adored focusing wholly and completely on his partner to the exclusion of all else. Could there really be any form of control more powerful than encasing his partner's cock within his muzzle? He could have kept the wolf there, balanced on the edge of orgasm, for hours upon hours if he so chose – or brought him swiftly over the edge, demonstrating to Charlie just how weak and soft he was in the face of lust.

Yes… There were so many different ways in which the moment could be played out, leaving every moment of control in his paws.

Exactly the way the fox wanted it.

He growled, sucking a little harder and bobbing his head up and down. Mimicking thrusts, though it had been a while indeed since Charlie had been inside the fox's rump, his cheeks hollowed faintly with the gentle force applied. The crème de la crème of the moment, however, came through in the teasing cup of his tongue dragging against the underside of the wolf's cock, Charlie's knot ever so slightly plumping out at the base of his cock. That was not something Kevin wanted to be inside his muzzle when the wolf hit his peak, for getting knotted in his mouth, well… It was hot to some, but not quite to him.

Not everything worked for every couple, after all. Yet he could linger there for a while longer as the sun continued its slow, patient dip towards the distant horizon. Not even the lapping of the waves on the ocean, becoming a little rougher and choppier as the wind picked up, could compare to the golden-red beauty, as much as the sea may have raged at time and tried to best the fiery orb. His ears flicked forward, pricking to attention, and the fox held back a grin around the wolf's cock the best he could.

Char was so obvious, quivering as he slipped closer to his high. The fox dragged his tongue around the head of his cock temptingly, squeezing it over every millimetre of sensitive flesh he found. After their years together, however, he knew the ins and out of Charlie's body intimately, though even Kevin felt there was fresh ground to be uncovered. Things changed, as always, and he liked the notion of always having something new to discover about his partner. It may have been boring otherwise.

"Mmm… Someone's getting close," he teased, drawing back and off Char's dick, pumping the length with his paw as he spoke. "I told you it wouldn't be long before you couldn't help yourself."

"You're just too good," the wolf panted, his long, pink tongue spilling hotly from his maw. "Mmmph… Please, don't leave me hanging."

"Oh," the fox said, kneeling up and peeling down his own trunks to expose his shaft. "But I thought you'd want me inside you first. At least, that's what I intend."

They may not have had lube, but it was okay for them both as they could take it slow – and, of course, stop if there was any trouble there. The wolf kicked off his shorts while the fox left his strained between his thighs, as if they were trying to keep his legs together. Kevin, however, had no reason to spread his legs for anyone at that time, lying back as Charlie straddled his hips, facing him.

They kept eye contact as Kevin dropped him a teasing wink, holding his throbbing shaft up as the wolf tried to sink on to him. It took a little finesse to get the slender head of his cock into the wolf's backside, although his cock was a shade smaller than Charlie's.

"Oof…"

As the head of his cock ground in, slowly, the fox watched Charlie's reactions carefully. He didn't want to go too fast or too hard, even if there was a time limit, though the idea of someone coming upon them while he was balls-deep inside Char's ass was rather an appealing notion too.

What would happen, he thought, if they really got caught? Would they be watched or would the one who caught them in the act back off, flushed and stumbling over their own hind paws to get free. He didn't know what would be better, though Kevin thought he would rather enjoy a spreading, hot blush that could be seen, faintly, through an anthro's fur. It wasn't something usually visible, but perhaps that was part of his heated arousal putting new fantasies into his mind.

The wolf's tail hole was tight around him as Charlie sank a little more and Kevin gripped his hips once his cock was inside. He didn't need to hold his cock up in position as he ground in, giving a little roll up with his hips just to sink another centimetre or so into the wolf's rump.

"Mmm… Oh, you feel as good as always, darling," the fox grunted, lips twitching as he fought to get his words out cleanly. "Can I cum inside? Less…mm…mess to clean up here. And always *better*."

His fingers curled around the wolf's cock as he hissed out the last words and Charlie moaned, too tongue-tied to even say anything in return. The fox's head fell back against the towel, some of the sand in his fur already, though Kevin could not bring himself to care. It was too good to be there in the moment, his skin prickling with tenacious heat, even as need built deep within his loins.

Kevin growled, needing it all, every drop of it. Yet the fox's attention slipped to his partner's cock, pumping it in time with the strokes of his shaft disappearing up into Char's asshole. The fox grunted in the back of his throat, though any sounds he made were easily overcome by the wolf's groans and whimpers, somehow teasing into a higher pitch than may otherwise have been expected.

"Oh… Ohhh…"

The wolf's head fell back, his throat quivering as the vulnerable, off-white expanse of it was shown off to his partner. Yet Char did not even know how beautiful he was in that moment, leaving Kevin, breathlessly, to bear witness to his moment of climax. As the wolf trembled to that very edge of orgasm, he pumped his cock increasingly swiftly, using a smear of Charlie's own pre-cum to lubricate his cock. It was something that may have been useful for them to have to help him slide into the wolf's tail hole, but taking things slow had been more than enough for them there. At least they knew one another intimately enough to understand how those little nuances played out between their bodies.

Charlie's chest rose, inflating with a sudden, sharp gasp of breath, though it did not seem to ease anything in him at all. For the wolf needed a very different kind of release as he huffed and panted, his tongue dangling wetly from his maw. If he'd been more with himself in the moment, he would have felt a little shy about the droplets of saliva splattering from his open mouth, although there was nothing to be done about it. Not as his knot swelled and Kevin gripped it tightly at just the right moment, sending the wolf howling over the edge with the sunset framing him in the background.

As he cried out his bliss, liquid passion painted Kevin's stomach and lower abdomen as the wolf creamed himself. It did not stop the wolf from rising and falling more desperately on Kevin's cock, however, dragging the fox right along with him, though that was right where the fox wanted to be.

He didn't even think of where they were and that they were out in the open, technically, no – not anymore. There was no need to, not as he heaved and panted heavily, snatching what breaths he could into his lungs while he had the chance. His stomach tensed, abs contracting, and he pushed up at the moment his knot pumped up, thick and tight with need, trembling there for a breathtaking moment before he unleashed all the cream he had to give.

Kevin was more restrained than the wolf, but he gripped his partner's hips hard to drag him all the way down on to his cock, bar the knot. Ah, that was a part of him that would have to be seated into the wolf's tail hole later on that night, once they were back in the hotel and relaxing together. Locking their bodies together in the aftermath of lust, after all, would not be the best idea when they were still down on the beach. Even if that would have been pretty hot too…

So, he erupted into the wolf's tail hole with raw abandon, letting Charlie grind down on to his cock as he huffed and panted, coming down slowly from his high. Pearly ropes of cum soaked into the fox's fur, though that would have to wait to be cleaned off later, the evidence of their tryst.

Above Kevin, the wolf wobbled, bracing himself with a paw on Kevin's shoulder as he threatened to collapse entirely on top of his partner. Yet it was not quite what the moment called for as the fox let out a strangled sort of groan, lips stretching into a goofy, open-mouthed smile as he spent every drop of cum he had to give into the wolf's backside. It drooled out softly around the join of their bodies, for they didn't have the knot to form a tight seal there, even if grinding on to a knot was one of Char's favourite things. That was partially why Kevin had played things out as he had too: all to see his partner lose it, quivering and moaning.

The wolf blushed and, more gently, curved down over the fox's body to kiss him. They slotted their muzzles together comfortably as Char tipped his head to the side, his tail lifting and wagging, even though his rump was still stuffed full. They could not stay on the beach for much longer but, with a rump full of cum, Charlie already surely had a few ideas in mind for just how their evening together could be played out, at the end of their little holiday.

As long as they were together, it didn't matter whether it was a beach day or just a day at home for them. It was their connection and intimacy that mattered, though sometimes it took getting away to refresh that.

Together, they'd always find exactly what they needed.

A Quick Fling

It was just a quick fling, I thought, as the bear pinned me to the wall, my hips pushing out instinctively, just wanting him close to me. I couldn't help it, not in how near I wanted him, his body covering mine, bigger and burlier, for I was only an English badger with white stripes marking my face. Some said they made me look older than I was, so perhaps the big Grizzly bear thought I was older than him and not within a couple of years of his age.

We'd met at one of the gay clubs in the city and it was funny really that we ran across each other as many times as we did. The city should have been too big for us to keep running into one another, but the gay scene there wasn't all that well developed and there were only so many places that furs like us could go to express ourselves. It was also good to remember when the gay culture and bars were the only places we could go to for safety and companionship too. History was a part of everything.

And so was being nudged less than gently into the backseat of the bear's car (at least, I assumed it was his car) as he took control, a smile on his muzzle that was ever so slightly cocky. He didn't need to be anything other than what he was, though he looked on the younger side too, maybe a couple of years younger than me, so that would put him in his early twenties rather than mid-twenties, like me.

I wished I could embody that, throwing all to the wind as if it no longer mattered. Dressed in ripped jeans and a sleeveless shirt, I couldn't decide quite whether the bear was trying too hard (hey, that was his right too) or if that was just his style. The sleeveless shirt, however, showed off the muscles in his arms nicely, even if they were softer with a layer of fat over them too. Everything about the brown-furred bear oozed raw power, though I didn't think he was trying to put on too much of a face and a front. He had his group of friends he hung out with, when I saw him, and seemed easy going at the very least.

And, he was always up to talk to others. I watched him slip out at strange times, though it was hardly unusual for furs to hook up at gay bars and the like. Still, it was not usually encouraged for furs to fuck in the bathrooms, the alleyways, car parks... Well, anywhere that could cause them trouble. Which made sense: it wasn't a place for sex. That didn't mean furs didn't do it, however.

His car, however, was parked a little way from the bar, down a side street that was quiet, perched between factory buildings. At the very least, it was secluded down there, though I still knew we had to be quiet, that there was only so much we could do.

We wanted each other and the bear growled, pinning me over the wide backseats as I grunted, rolling my hips up to him. My shaft ached and throbbed, sliding too quickly from the fleshy tuck of my sheath, desperate for attention. Yet perhaps I just wanted something the bear had been teasing me with for weeks already.

I knew his name, even though he hadn't given it to me: Tyrion. That was a pretty cool name, though I was sure he didn't know my name. And neither did the bear need to know my name as his sharp, predatory teeth nipped and caught at the fur of my neck.

"Mmm... Oh, fuck..."

The hiss escaped me in a rush of breath, though I was comfortable there, even with the harder backseat of the car (at least something big enough for the bear to drive and ride in comfortably) pressing up into my back. I huffed, puffing out my cheeks with air, but then he had his lips on mine, a low, almost dominant growl rolling from him.

Maybe he wasn't experienced enough to be dominant though. But the moment was all about taking what we wanted from each other, no more than that.

The kiss, however… It was everything. Everything I might have imagined it to be in a quick dalliance like that, grunting in the back of my throat, our tongues twisting and curling, trying their best to flick up against one another. Our muzzles, at the very least, were something we were familiar with, a similar shape. That helped, for kissing anthros with very differently shaped muzzles and lips – even beaks, furs with bigger teeth and more – could be quite challenging at times.

His paw slid down my body, tugging at my shirt, and I was not cold at all, even if it had been a grey sort of day, a bit drizzly, before night had fallen. It was not the kind of weather, to be fair, to be heading out to clubs at all, but I'd needed that company and the sneaky thrill of seeing Tyrion again, even if the bear probably didn't know I looked for him every time I went out. Most of the time, I caught at least a glimpse of him.

His paw grabbed at my crotch, a little crude and a little rough, and I was abruptly glad of the cool air wrapping around us, the car door still open to the bear's back, his bulk blocking the way.

The bear kneaded more softly over my crotch, feeling the outline of my aching hard-on. It swelled thickly into his paw, his fingers trying to curl all the way around my length even while I still had my clothes on but, well…it didn't seem that was going to take all that much longer, not with how he was groping me like that.

Fuck… I couldn't wait to feel his hardness grinding into me too, how thick and it was going to be. As much as I'd fantasised about the bear, I'd never been able to fill in the mental details of his cock in my mind.

But all that was going to change soon as he palmed my cock and kissed me more crudely, seeming to test my readiness with the fervent push and press of his tongue inside my mouth. He didn't force my tongue out of the way, no, but experimentally dominating, filling more of my mouth with his tongue than was the case the other way around. And that was okay with me, all but melting into his touch.

With all I believed he had in mind, I really would have let the Grizzly bear do anything to me, anything at all he wanted.

He broke the kiss with a wet pant, warm, moist breath tickling my muzzle, the shorter, almost coarser fur there. Of course, I kept my fur in good condition, but it wasn't the kind of romp where Tyrion was going to be holding my face tenderly and stroking my muzzle, oh on. I would well have been disappointed if it was.

Not all sex had to be sweet.

"Mm, didn't think you'd be hard already," he hissed out through his teeth, breaking the kiss. "That's hot."

"Unff…"

I wanted to say something, but all I could get to break my lips was a groan. It was just too good as he drew back, tugging at the waistband of my trousers, the belt I'd put on to hold them up. There was a little pin in it, that I'd got from an animal sanctuary at some point, but it was probably too dark for the Grizzly to realise it had the mark of a bear's paw on it. Maybe that was a little sign, at least to me, that everything was meant to be.

But I couldn't put too flowery a spin on it, as much as I may have liked to think the threads of fate brought everything together, one way or another. No… Yet I could slink down into the tenor of the moment, relishing in every small sensation.

The brush of his fingers on my zipper, pulling it down.

How he hissed out through his teeth, a little shudder going through him.

The press of my cock up against my underwear, though it no longer even mattered what I was wearing.

He pulled my trousers down and exposed my shaft, the bulge of it tenting up through my underwear. But the bear was not satisfied with that and, honestly, I would have been disappointed if he was. I wanted so much from him and my expectations, most likely, were higher than they should have been, though I had to try, I had to lust, I had to see what was there, one way or the other.

"Mmmph... Ah... Fuck..."

I managed to grunt out a single word, though that was more than enough for him as he smirked, his teeth glinting white in the sheen of a nearby lamppost. It was not that close, however, so his features were only softly illuminated, even if I swore there was a different warmth in his brown eyes.

I didn't want to lose myself in those pools of brown, his eyes with more depth to them now, up close and personal. I might never have come back from them ever again, if that was the case.

His ears twitched, the light prickle of drizzling rain alighting on his fur, forming tiny droplets. I don't know why that was what my attention clung to as I kicked down my trousers and he helped me out of them, though that left me terribly exposed out there in the open air.

My tail twitched as it was exposed, though there was enough fluff around the underside of it and around my rump to cover my pucker from view. That was what the bear was after, even if head at the side of the car may have been a smarter thing to go for, at least straight away.

But we could and would take whatever it was we craved, heat pooling between us with the tingle of late-night drizzle to cool us, at least a little. He didn't have to expose himself, though he worked single-pawed to tug his jeans down, unzipping them and tugging out his hardening cock. It sprung out into the grasp of his paw and the bear grunted thickly, a deep, guttural sound, as he stroked it. It seemed to be near full hardness already, though the head of his cock was defined and not at all like what I had thought, when trying to imagine, what his cock would be like.

The glands at the head had a defined, smooth shape with a rounded tip, the slit bubbling pre-cum – but he couldn't be that overly productive, could he? As I grunted and slipped a bit lower back against the car seats, I caught another bubble of pre-cum rising from the slit at the head of his cock.

Damn… Maybe he really has that much to give.

I tried to get a sneaky look at his balls, but I only got a glimpse, even if they had to be big and full, at least to be as leaky as he was. It was hot, however, and I reached for him as he pushed over me, bending my legs back a little.

I took the cue and bent my knees, though they, of course, would not go all the way back to my chest. That was crazy! Few were that flexible and, well, I was not the kind of switch who was overly fit and stretchy when it came to the physical capabilities of my body. It was enough, however, more than enough for him to get in close as his cock ground into the fur of my backside.

"Mmmm… Ah, come on," I groaned, haste layering my tone, even if I may have wanted to savour the moment too. "Get on with it, sheesh…"

Under my breath, I muttered.

"I've been waiting for this for too long."

I don't think he caught that last bit, for it came out in a whisper of breath, but that was as it was meant to be too. I didn't want to expose everything to him, not all like that, for I most likely would not see him after that night.

I'd take everything he had for me, however, all he had to give me. And that was fine, for life was about those little moments, how everything was supposed to come together – not always sweetly but in a patchwork of experiences.

His cock grinding into my rump was just due to him shifting position, though I didn't mind that. It was just another little note that I could sink into the moment of, cool air brushing my nose as I inhaled deeply.

A plethora of scents assaulted my nose as I let out a low groan, so soft and breathy that perhaps it need not have been said at all. Yet the crisp, night air came tainted with a hint of oil and exhaust fumes, the smell of the kebab shop that I think was around the corner too. It was Tyrion himself, however, that I wanted to take in, inhaling too deeply again, my chest expanding; I was sure he noticed.

But his musk spray into an undertone to the cacophony of aromas pulling at my attention, a musky, earthen scent that, to be fair, came edged with a hint of sweat too. It had been fairly warm within the club, of course, with that many bodies all bunched up in there, but there was something spicy in his scent too, which I could only catch when I breathed in fully, taking a bigger lungful of air than usual.

That scent would be locked into my memory forevermore as he pushed into me, grinding his cock into the fur of my rump, a trail of slick pre-cum smearing in its wake. I didn't know how it was possible for him to drip and drool as much as he was, though he dipped his cock a bit lower, pressing the head up to the bud of my tail hole.

"Mmm... Been a while since I've done this," he grunted, smirking down at me, though I wondered if there was something more vulnerable in his gaze too, something a little shakier. "Fuck, you're hot..."

I parted my lips to say something, but he did too good a job of stealing those very words from my lips as he ground against my tail hole, having found the entrance he was looking for. My fluffy, dense fur didn't help much there, but it was okay, for he was in control and, that time, it was up to Tyrion to find my tail hole and thrust.

Pre-cum dripped coolly against my anal ring as he paused there, the moment seeming to draw out forever. And yet I couldn't think of anything else at all besides how good it felt to have him against me, his body warming against mine.

Slowly, he pushed in, his eyes on me, burning with an intensity I didn't know he had in him. Yet there was a lot I didn't know about the bear and so much yet to learn.

"Mmmm... Ah!"

I gasped, short and sharp, the intake of breath biting in my chest, though only for a moment. It needed no more time than that to make itself known, the press of his aching member inside me spreading me open, slowly. We could have taken more time to get ready and prepare, but there was only so much, in that instance, we could and would do.

Not when the height of need was so great my blood sang with need and lust, my whole body seeming to pump and pulse with the kind of energy I had to pay mind to, one way or another. I groaned, lips parted, no longer as quiet as I should have been, though that didn't matter. It was too good with him pressing over me, his body covering mine, the outside world blocked out but for the bulk of the bear's body. It was not like when he had been standing in the car doorway, no, but more softly dominating, though there was no longer a casual sense to the moment.

And that was okay as he pumped inside me, grinding deeper and deeper, my body sucking around every millimetre he had to offer, feeling it all intimately – perhaps a little too intimately. My body stretched around him, though I really had to concentrate to not clench on to his cock. It was just too tempting, wanting to squeeze, to get a little more pressure, even though it already felt as if his cock was more than large enough for me.

I groaned, eyelids fluttering, though it had been a long time since I had felt pressure and pleasure like that, something that made me want to sink into the moment even more, settling there. I panted heavily, tongue fluttering between my teeth, though it was more usual for me to breathe through my nose. I just wanted to take everything in, how big he was – and how tender he was too, even if that did not quite feel right for what we were doing and where we were fucking.

It wasn't supposed to be sweet and yet… he took it slowly. He could have taken his own pleasure in paw alone and thrust harder and faster, slamming into me roughly – and I would have liked that too. But I liked how he was fucking me even more in that moment, the deep, penetrating grind of his cock rooting me there, pinning me into the backseats. It was a vulnerable position to be in, that much was sure, though I didn't feel as if I was in a compromising position in the slightest. Perhaps it was not quite a safe position, but it was a better position to be in.

If anyone came by, after all, they'd see him first, not me. At least that may well be time enough for me to cover up my crotch, though I doubted we'd even stop even if someone scurried by.

With the bear, his hardness driving into me, I panted heavily, trying to thrust back at him but not really managing more than that. A clench of muscles in my body, contracting where I was not quite able to control myself, was all I had to give, tightening around him in the meantime.

"Ah… Oh!"

The effect on the bear was electric and I paused for a moment, breath tight in my chest, studying him. He really was resplendent, despite the crudity of our situation, tall and broad, with a wide chest that begged attention. I imagined my paws running over his pecs and down to his thicker muscle-gut repeatedly.

Maybe that would have to stay in my imagination, however. But that was okay as I watched him, all the little twitches in his body, how his damp fur was rimmed with a faint sheen of light, illuminating all the droplets clinging to him, though the drizzle was slowly dampening his head and neck especially. The bear was not as exposed as I was, although the moment was right, my naked ass pushed up so he could bear down into my tail hole at just the right angle.

It was right, however, for him to be wearing more clothes than me, though perhaps we could have remained more discreet if I had bent over in the car with my ass thrust back at him. Then my backside would have just been on show and my clothes wouldn't have had to be pulled off. Speaking of which, I wasn't at all sure where my boots had ended up, though that was something to be worried about later, when I had to head back home after everything.

"Unff…"

The bear leaned further over me, pressing my legs back closer to my chest as he sought a deeper angle in which to thrust, my tail hole twitching and pulling lightly around him, as much as I tried to relax. Yet it was not about doing everything perfectly but taking the moment for what it was, hissing out a breath through my teeth with his long, slow thrusts. Every grind of his cock into my ass felt like it was going deeper than before, though it was impossible to tell just how deep he was inside me, despite him having a very sizeable cock on him.

It was a miracle it had gone inside me as it had, but it was all down to the bear and how he treated me, how he ground in slowly, letting my body adjust. Yet it had all seemed to happen so quickly, despite everything.

"Mmmm…"

I rolled my head back against the seats, a puff of air escaping my lips. I wondered what the bear saw in me, a badger stuck in his car, impaled on his cock, though it did not truly matter. Yet there was a small part of me that wanted to know still, to have his perspective on matters.

Stop thinking about that.

Sometimes, I over thought things. But the bear made it easier as he ground into me, the deep, steady pump of his hips a rhythm I could focus on. Finally, his hips ground up against my backside, no more distance between us, and he pressed in as deep as he could, a hiss rolling from his lips.

He panted heavily, though no words were needed as we both relished in that moment, that deepest penetration. His furry balls seemed to have slipped out of his clothes as they bumped against my backside, lightly jostling each other, though I didn't mind at all.

All I wanted was that closeness, that moment of intimacy with a stranger that I had never anticipated coming, not like that. Not before that day, not even as I grunted softly and tried to roll my hips up to him, wanting more.

"Ah… Please…"

I needed him to fuck me, to take me, for my own need had been set aside, at least for the moment. But that was okay, as his paw brushed over my cock, and he did just what I could not say aloud, thrusting shortly and sharply, grinding into me with cruder, more desperate strokes than before.

It seemed I was getting to him too, though that was purely me speculating, for I could not know, not truly. He panted more heavily, the pace of his thrusts speeding up, grunts mingling with the slap of his hips against my ass, as much as the sound was muted by our fur. So many sharper, harder edges of our bodies were softened by that coat of fur, a little thicker on both of us to get us through the winter (if we were still living like our ancestors) but I felt every inch of him I needed to.

My cock throbbed, aching against my lower abdomen, though it was not fully hard, not in that moment. It was difficult to remain like that with anal penetration, at least for me, though that was different for everyone.

Maybe I'd get off after or maybe I wouldn't, but I languished there as he thrust harder and faster, the pump of his hips tinged with that brutal edge I needed from him.

"Mmph… Ah, fuck, yes…"

"Nngghh…" He groaned, still thrusting as the bear breathlessly forced words from his lips. "Not gonna…last much longer…"

It seemed to take a great effort just for him to get those words out and I moaned my acceptance of that. I didn't want him to hold out, not just for me, but to fill me with every drop of cum his nuts had to give. I couldn't feel him leaking anymore, lacking that kind of sensation within my anal passage, but there would be a lot more of that slick deluge, I thought, if he was anything as productive as he had been with the sheer volume of pre-cum he made.

Fuck, that was hot… Hotter than, honestly, it had any right to be, even then. He thrust harder and faster, grinding in deep as if he was trying to use every last bit of my tail hole he had access to. The press of his muscle gut against my legs locked me into position and I wouldn't have been able to get away from him even if I'd not been trapped in the car.

It was rough and tasteful, something that would remain in my memory for a long time after that night on its own. Yet that night was never meant to stand alone as he huffed hotly and crammed his cock deep, a rapid, shuddering reverberation suddenly going through him. I should have expected that, however, panting heavily while he slammed in deep, staying there while he spent his load inside me.

I imagined I could feel it splashing up inside, so hot and creamy – but I didn't have to imagine when there was even more seed leaking out around his cock, even though I'd thought the seal of my ass and his cock had been so tight that surely nothing could seep down the length of it. He panted heavily, tongue pressing out against his lips in a swift swipe before retreating back into the dark cavern of his maw. Clenching around his shaft in one of the final squeezes I would get, I leaned into the moment, committing it to memory.

From the brush of his fur against my rump to the way his paw crept back up my abdomen, to my cock, it was all there. My own shaft throbbed anxiously, wanting my orgasm, though I thought that would have to wait. Cum marked the rim of my tail hole, cooling to the glint of the air, but I stayed there, moaning softly, letting him take all he needed from me.

At least, until his paw curled around my cock as if my dick was meant to fit within the grasp of his paw. I gasped, eyes wide open again, though that only revealed the bear filling my vision, not able to get down to my muzzle again but close enough as his warm breath tickled my fur.

"Ah, what are you..." I tried to force out the words, my stomach lurching, though not unpleasantly. "Mmmph... What are you doing?"

"Taking care of you too," he said simply, having caught his breath by that point. "Mmmph... Fuck, you're hot... Never've cum that quick after drinks before."

I whimpered throatily, surprised by the pitch of the sound that broke my lips, though I had to let it cum, stroke my stroke, my shaft aching into his paw. I tried to say something about it not being necessary, feeling my exposure, but it was not worth forcing the words out when my whole body sung for orgasm as it did.

He stroked my cock, my shaft smaller than his by a couple of inches and definitely slimmer, though it was still a moderate size. And that only meant it was a good size to fit his paw, sliding up and down, pulling the skin lightly along with the passage of his paw. I panted, lips parted, saliva evaporating swiftly from them as my mouth was rendered entirely too dry as I dragged in every gasp of sweet air I could.

I just had to hold on, to let pleasure swamp me, rising through my body as if I was being filled up with liquid lust. I was warm, too warm – and by far a lot closer to orgasm than I had realised. That was okay though, at least I thought, grunting as he pawed me off, a smirk on his lips.

I stared at him as climax gripped me, that pinnacle edging me for seemingly forever. Yet it was just adrenaline pumping through me, sirens going off in the distance, though there was no one nearby, thankfully, to catch us in the act. Not as I leaned into climax, a ragged groan ripping from my muzzle that didn't sound as if it belonged there, huffing and panting, spurts of cum shooting over my lower abdomen. Some spurts even reached my shirt, staining the hemline, though I was not as productive as the bear had been, his cock softening within my tail hole even then.

It was only a shame he could not stuff me for longer, his cock slipping out in a messy spill of cum, a cream-pie marking my tail hole as it soaked into my fur, thick and gooey. I moaned and slumped into the seats, losing any tension I'd been holding in my body, letting it all happen, regardless of the mess. And there were no words I could put to that euphoria, how it flowed and pulsed through me, even if it was over more swiftly than I would have liked it to be. Such was the way of orgasm, at least for a guy…but I'd take it when I had not expected to cum in there, the delicious note topping off the entire experience as Tyrion looked down at me. In hindsight, I thought his expression was a little conflicted. We'd both got what we wanted from the experience though.

We'd have to part, re-dressing hastily and grunting our goodbyes, though there was no part of me that would ever regret the experience.

Later, however, when I found a card of his, which linked him to his job but still had his phone number on it, tucked into the back pocket of my trousers, I could not help but smile, lips twitching up lightly.

Maybe there was something more to a quick fling, or maybe it would fizzle as swiftly as it sparked up.

The only way to find out was to make the call and take the plunge.

Camping

"Mm, it's nice to be out here with you."

Guy exhaled softly, leaning back on the sleeping bags, which they'd pulled out near the campfire, with his partner beside him. The fox's red brush swished lazily to the side, teasing against Rhys' long, brown tail, though the Harris hawk rarely allowed others to touch his tail. For him, it was a very sensitive spot – and that much Guy could certainly appreciate.

Guy's fur was on the darker side to most anthros, a rich, dark red that came with streaks of black in it. In the right light, or dim light, he could look brown at times, although that never bothered Guy. The tip of his tail did not come with the typical white of many red foxes but was a darker black-brown, hinting at a touch of different heritage in his lineage. There was less white on his chest and belly than with most foxes, but the details of his body were not something Guy paid all that much attention to.

Rhys, on the other hand, well… Guy would have spent all day taking in every last little detail of the hawk's body, adoring every feather on the avian's body. It was almost an act of meditation to help the Harris hawk with the act of preening, smoothing down and teasing oil into every single feather on the bird's body as an act of worship in itself. That was, perhaps, not something Guy would have said aloud, though he didn't mind in the slightest that he was rather head over heels for the bird.

"It is nice, isn't it?" Rhys said as if he was drowsy, his dark beak parting slowly, eyes glinting with a predator's delight. "I'm glad you came out here with me, I didn't think we'd ever get a spare weekend to camp."

The Harris hawk looked down at his partner, his pupils drifting down to look at the top of the dark fox's ears. They twitched just below his beak and the sudden urge struck the avian to nip at them.

That wouldn't get him anywhere, however, not as he shifted his weight, settling Guy's head a little more comfortably on his chest as they lay back. There was nothing quite like looking up at the stars, the vast expanse of the cosmos, and realising just how small he was. To share that with his partner also was something special indeed, though he didn't think Guy saw things in quite the same manner as him.

They didn't have to have all the same perspectives and opinions, however, and could simply be themselves with one another. That was all either had ever really asked of a partner.

Guy, however, nuzzled up and under his chin, though the fox glowed with gratitude that the night was warm enough in the middle of summer for him to be in just a T-shirt and a loose pair of shorts. He'd gone without underwear, that time, though it wasn't something Guy paid all that much attention to.

The hawk, however, didn't feel the cold as the fox did and was bare-chested, allowing Guy to trace down over his feathers with the tip of his damp nose. Guy breathed slowly and evenly, inviting the hawk to match his breathing pattern. Settling back a little more with a soft sigh, the avian fanned out his tail feathers, fluttering them lightly as he twitched the long length of his tail, softly, back and forth. He may have only moved it a couple of inches at a time, if even that, but it relaxed him, sending a ripple all the way back up his spine.

The fox, however, had something of an ulterior motive there, ears twitching as the wind rustled through the pine trees. They'd made camp halfway up a hill, where there was a little, flat plateau for their tent to be pegged into safely, and a spot for them to set up the campfire. Although they'd dragged in logs to sit on, they had camp chairs too and, really, snuggling up together on top of a sleeping bag seemed far more appealing to them both.

It was that simple touch of physical contact that brought them closer together than ever, taking a break away from the real world to reconnect. Guy's tail lifted a little as he kissed the underside of Rhys' beak, though he couldn't help but push in a little nearer, his fingers sliding down the bird's chest to his midsection, curling lightly around his waist.

"Hm…" Rhys looked down at him, clicking the edges of his beak lightly together. "What are you doing down there?"

Guy blinked wickedly, affecting a look that was a side too innocent to be truly so.

"Nothing…"

He dragged the word out, nuzzling down, his warm breath tickling the hawk's feathers. Oh, he would never have done anything Rhys did not want and he knew where the lines were too.

Still, he could tempt and tease and see just what he could get out of the hawk.

Rhys murmured softly as the fox worked his way gently across his chest, nibbling and preening with his tongue and lips. Sometimes, his teeth came into play too, skilfully paying personal, intimate attention to his partner in a way that Rhys could only ever have imagined before. Yet that was just part of the moment, the hawk's mind going blank as his body quivered, feathers trying to ruffle even as the fox softly smoothed them down.

"Mmm…"

Rhys hummed happily, letting himself relax as Guy settled over him, sort of on all fours, paying complete attention to his body. They didn't have to say anything more in the moment, not as the fox exhaled, letting that light wash of breath pour over the brown feathers.

"You keep these in such good condition," Guy murmured, though he was only distracting Rhys as his paws slipped lower still, all the way down to the hawk's hips. "But you should let me preen you more, I heard of this amazing oil that does…wonders…"

His attention drifted, however, as he hooked his fingers, complete with the short, filed claws at the tip, into the top of the hawk's trousers, just past the waistband. They had an elastic waistband, for comfort in the evening, and were easy enough to slide down, though they weren't hiding anything at that time.

For the hawk did not, of course, have a sheath and balls like the fox, but only a slit where his shaft emerged from. It was a cloaca, but Guy wasn't focusing on nuzzling down inside the slit with his long, flexible tongue that time. All the fox wanted was to coax out the treat of his partner's cock, all to show Rhys exactly how much the hawk meant to him.

Rhys quivered, half propping up his torso as he grunted and blushed a little. His feathers hid it from view, though he felt it acutely in the chill of the night air.

It was too inviting to pause there and watch his partner, however, starlight glinting faintly off the edges of the fox's ears as if he had a halo around him. Guy moaned softly, so lightly that it could have been missed if Rhys was not paying close attention to it, though the moment was theirs to take as they pleased.

With complete solitude ringing around them, allowing them to settle in the wilderness, they could finally let go of everything that had been holding them down. There was no room for it out there, worries and trials, and they could finally focus on one another, boiling their experience down to sensation and intimacy: the anthro experience. All while love warmed them through, lifting them whenever their spirits dipped even in the slightest.

"Mmm… I think you're up to something," Rhys said playfully, though there was a hitch in his voice as he tried to keep his tone level and even. "And you need no explanation."

"What?"

The fox blinked up at him, eyes half-lidded and his pink tongue lolling playfully. The fire flickered and danced, crackling as it snapped up the smaller twigs they'd fed it, but it seemed making s'mores would have to wait.

Rhys' cock pushed out of his cloaca slowly, parting his slit to reveal the slick, slightly curved length. It had a smooth undulation in the shaft, with the tip twisting back to ever so slightly point in the opposite direction, but it had the effect of balancing out the shape of the bird's shaft very nicely. Not that Guy was ever going to be comparing the Harris hawk's cock to anyone else's, though the fox could always show his appreciation of it.

He nuzzled into it, teasing the edges of the hawk's slit with his fingertips. It only took small movements of his fingers to dig into the sensitive flesh, barely even putting any pressure on him in the slightest. Guy sucked in a breath, the wash of his exhale tickling over Rhys' shaft, though he caught the shudder rippling through the hawk all the same.

He knew exactly what he was doing and made no apology for it as he kneaded faintly and massaged around the hawk's rising shaft, letting the length push up against his lips. Guy didn't have to do anything specific, parting his lips and allowing the tip to tuck itself into his mouth. He grunted around the firm length pushing into his maw, groaning lightly in the back of his throat, for all those little things, like the vibrations from his lips, played into the moment he wanted to show Guy.

And that was a moment where only the two of them existed, no one more. They could have been the only two, completely and truly, left in the world – and he may well have been happy with that too. He needed that break from a time where he was always expected to be doing something or living up to someone else's expectations and if he could give that to Rhys too, what else could he ever hope for?

So, the fox languished there, letting the moment come slowly, for there was no rush to be had between them. The cooling air of the night would not chill them in the summer months, even if the sky was clear: it still proved to be a welcome respite after the moderate heat of the day. Guy murmured around Rhys' cock as he took it deep, sliding the seven-inch length, give or take a smidge, into his foxy muzzle.

A fox's muzzle, after all, was much better at sucking cock than a bird's beak was – and that was something Rhys was just going to have to own up to, at some point. Not that Guy was the sort to rub it in, no, not in the slightest, but he was rather proud, conversely, of his cock sucking abilities. Especially when the avian shuddered under him with a strangled screech, as much as the Harris hawk swallowed it down and tried to hide it.

"Mmmm..." He mumbled around the avian's cock, though Guy perhaps should not have been talking. "I love when you do...that..."

Yet sucking dick took up more of his attention, even though that was quite a crude way to put it. Sometimes loving things could be lewd and there was nothing wrong with that, though Guy was not always the sort to soften his language when he was caught up in the heat of the moment. It was simply difficult to think of anything else as he bobbed his muzzle, taking in the full length and dragging his lips and tongue sensually back to caress Rhys' cock.

The hawk trembled and moaned, though there was no reason for him to hold back his cries in a moment like that, no, not at all. Still, there was some part of Rhys that said he had to be quieter, that there was a risk someone could hear him – but he wasn't back in his flat anymore, no. That had boasted rather thin walls and getting heard in the throes of passion was very much a risk back there.

That was why camping had appealed to them initially, though it had taken a while to get both of them out there. The avian ruffled his feathers and rested his hand on the back of the fox's head, trying to relax even as lines of tension thrummed through his body.

"Mmph…"

It was difficult, Rhys grunting in the back of his throat, pressing the edges of his beak together too harshly for comfort. Yet the facial muscles twitching and aching weren't enough to stop him from savouring the moment, trying to absorb every little moment as his hips shifted lightly from one side to the other and back again.

The fox sank into it as he traced his tongue lightly against the underside of the hawk's cock, playing back and forth with him. There were many things a long, flexible tongue like that could do and he groaned lightly, pushing his muzzle all the way down to the base of Rhys' cock. The very tip of his tongue poked out, trapped between the hawk's dick and his bottom lip, though no one was there to bear witness to that goofy little note.

Everything was as it needed to be as he curled and lashed his tongue around as much of that smooth, gently curved length as he could. The aroma of male musk sank into him, though there was a distinct scent from the hawk's feathers too. It was not so much of a dusty smell but carried a hint of the natural oils Rhys' body produced too, something that would always be inherently a part of the Harris hawk.

If he was ever without the hawk, Guy would go to sleep with his nose buried in the hawk's pillow, or at least on his side of the bed, all so he could linger in the scent of his beloved. Scent held somewhat less importance to avians, but it would always be one of the penultimate things to a fox like Guy.

However, he was surprised when the Harris hawk pulled him up a little, drawing his muzzle from that aching length of cock. Guy groaned, tail lifting, blinking blearily as he tried to catch on to what was happening in the moment, panting lightly.

"Mmm, what's going on?" He grunted, working his jaw a little and running his tongue around his lips. "What're you thinking, Rhys?"

The hawk, however, tipped his muzzle up, curling his fingers lightly around the underside. His eyes bore warmly into the fox's and, for a breath of a moment, the fox felt his heart skip a beat.

Oh, why did the Harris hawk always do that to him? Just a look from the hawk... Well, it changed everything for him, absolutely everything. And he never wanted to go back to any kind of existence without the bird.

Rhys smirked faintly, showing it in his eyes as, of course, his beak couldn't form the expression. He took Guy into his arms and pulled him close, though the press of the fox's clothes against his bare feathers just wasn't what he was looking for.

"Ah, you didn't think I was going to let you get away with just pleasing me, did you?" Rhys said playfully, twisting the fox around so his chest gently pushed down to the now slightly messed up sleeping bag. "That's not how things go between us, hon... You know that."

"Mmph..." Guy grunted. "You know... I like doing that stuff for you too."

"But you're going to let me take care of you."

Even though the two of them were happy enough to swap roles back and forth, it always gave Guy a special kind of thrill when Rhys took charge. The hawk pushed him lightly down, helping him get his arms up over his head so he could help the fox out of his shirt, though his shorts were easier. In usual form for when he was enjoying more casual clothing, Guy had gone without underwear that day, freeing his sheath and growing shaft for Rhys' attention.

"Mmm, see, I knew you were holding out on me," Rhys teased lightly, stroking his fingers up the underside of the fox's cock to the tip. "You didn't have to set yourself aside for me, darling, don't you worry about anything like that."

Guy groaned and nodded, sort of on all fours but with his chest tipped more down towards the ground. He panted heavily, letting his partner take care of him, though it felt a little strange that time. That said, he had been pulled from the task of cock sucking that he really enjoyed too.

His shorts eased off all the way as Rhys took care of that too, leaving them both completely bare, from head to toe. He quivered there, letting his body rest more heavily on his upper chest, pushing his weight increasingly to his right shoulder.

Guy groaned, however, as Rhys settled in behind him, the crackle and snap of the fire to their backs at least warming them through. He shivered, though he was not cold, as the bird ran the curve of his beak over his buttocks, teasing with the faintest of pressure. To the fox who wanted so much more than that, it was the sweetest kind of torture.

"Mmmm…"

"Take it easy, fox," the bird soothed, though the feathers on his wing-like arms fluttered softly as he eased down. "I've got you."

So, Guy trusted him – just from those simple words alone. There was nothing else he needed than to be with the Harris hawk, losing himself there as the avian pressed in closer and let his tongue slip out against the pucker of the fox's tail hole. Guy groaned, tongue flicking out against his lips, though did his best to contain himself.

That, however, was more of a trial than ever with a partner who knew him as deeply and as intimately as Rhys did. The hawk only had to make the tiniest of motions with his tongue, digging his talon-like fingers lightly into the fox's buttocks. He didn't technically need to spread Guy's rear cheeks for the moment, but he leaned into it all the same, just for that extra sensation and pleasure it gave them both.

Guy groaned, a shivering mess of a fox from that alone. The hawk traced his tongue lightly against his anal ring, dipping inside smoothly, as if his tongue was made from silk. It all came so easily to Rhys, as if the avian didn't have to think about it at all, the fox's tail readily lifting for him. Guy couldn't have pushed it down if he'd tried to, though all he wanted was for his partner to have his way with him.

If only he had the words with which to articulate that…

"Mmmm… Please…"

Guy tried anyway, panting heavily, his chest heaving for every hard-won breath. Rhys shushed him quietly, rubbing his backside briefly before returning to his work.

Rimming was not something for every partner, but it was something that suited how they liked to best enjoy one another. He took his time with the fox, minutes ticking by as he slowly ate out his musky yet fresh tail hole. The only scent lingering there, of course, was from the fox's natural aroma, though the hawk's attention only briefly flicked to it. It didn't need to be the highlight of the moment when texture was so much more important to Rhys. The lines and ripples in the fox's pucker entranced him – and even more so the tighter, hotter heat within his anal passage.

Rhys could have spent all day there with his tongue pressed up into the fox's tail hole, feeling it twitch and pull around him. The fox was barely in control of himself, whimpering and moaning as he drooled just a little too heavily, though a little mess was no trouble at all to either of them. Any clenching came from Guy, mostly, but any other little twitches and tugs of muscles were simply a product of the moment, something his body ached for and showed so very openly.

That was not a bad thing in the slightest, not as he moaned against the fox and pressed the curve of his beak up between the fox's rear cheeks. Guy's tail pushed over his head, hanging there, though Rhys relaxed into the sensation, even if it was a little too warm with that thick brush simply dangling there.

He pawed at Guy's cock, closing his fingers around it – though he didn't really need to jack off his partner at the same time, for the fox was already so caught up in the moment that he was rock hard and ready. He stroked up and down slowly, teasing the length and smearing the dribble of pre-cum down it. That time, however, they would not need any greater lubrication than that.

There was lube in the tent, of course, with their kit, though neither fox nor hawk wanted to fetch it. Guy moaned, trying to form words, though the fox was barely even able to string words together into something of a coherent thought. It didn't matter, not as the hawk withdrew slightly, resting his chin on top of the fox's ass, lazily stroking his cock.

"I think you're ready for me," he murmured, taking a more important moment to check in with Guy. "Are you? Do you want my cock? Or shall we do something else?"

"Ah…" Guy moaned, trying to rock his hips back against the bird, though the Harris hawk easily moved with him, predicting his movements as if he was perfectly in-tune with his body. "What… Ah, no… Want you…in me…"

He hoped that was what the hawk was asking him, but, well, it was not as if Guy wasn't making his wants and needs known in the moment – which was one of the most important aspects of communication during sex. He licked his lips and glanced back, his gaze grazing that of the hawk's as Rhys adjusted position.

Seamlessly, though perhaps not as fluidly as they would have if all was perfect, they shuffled into another position, though it was unlike Guy to take such a bottom position. He lay on his back, head on the sleeping bag and the rest of his body on the grass. There was a little give to the earth under him as he flattened the grass with his weight, so it was not an uncomfortable position, though he was a fox who more often was aligned with home comforts. What was the point in working hard, after all, if he didn't get a little luxury?

But the hawk took up position between his spread legs, hooking them up around his waist, as if

Rhys knew exactly what it was the fox wanted, even without Guy saying anything at al. The fox whined plaintively, the scent of fresh grass tickling his nose as some of the blades were crushed under his back. Even the act of stirring up the grass wafted the scent around them, the warm seduction of the night flowing around him.

"Please…" He breathed, looking up at Rhys as if the hawk was the only one in the world to him. "I need you… Now."

He shook his head slowly and whimpered his permission. The hawk was not in any position to lean over his body, closing the distance between them, though there would be plenty more time to enjoy cuddling later that night. He smiled, however, his eyes warming and his beak parting, letting Guy know he was there for him, always there for him.

There was no difference between them, not as the hawk, slowly, slid into the fox's backside. It all began with a teasing press of the slimmer tip of his cock up to Guy's tail hole, enjoying the pulse of that twitching pucker for a heartbeat of a moment before applying pressure. There was no rush, after all, and between the two of them there would never be.

So, he allowed the weight of his body to guide him deeper, sliding inch after inch of his faintly throbbing cock into the fox's body. Guy squeezed around him, letting out a strangled kind of howl as he flung his arms back and up over his head, shuddering on the luxuriously impaling spire of the hawk's shaft.

"Mmm… Ohhhh, yessss…"

Guy couldn't stop himself from whimpering and whining – far louder than he ever had before. It was as if something changed for him in the sexual aspects, at least, of their relationship on that camping trip, though just how deeply those cords ran would only come to be seen as time passed. It would all prove to be for the better, however, allowing them to enjoy the moment of penetration and take it exactly as it was.

It didn't need to be any more than that, after all.

Guy hissed through his teeth and arched his back, locking his legs around the hawk's waist the moment he sank deeply enough into him. It was the only place he wanted to be, grunting in the back of his throat, even rolling his head and twisting from side to side as he fought to restrain himself. Yet there was nothing there to restrain him, least of all Rhys, and the hawk rubbed his leg soothingly as he rocked his hips, powering into the fox with smooth, devouring strokes. It was as if he was laying his claim to the fox all over again, though they were already each other's one and only.

The fox whined, though cut off the sound as his own cock throbbed, drooling pre-cum. It was not fully hard, not with the pressure of penetration, but that was okay. It didn't mean he wouldn't be able to reach his high in the slightest and he was quite happy with things just as they were. His knot tried to inflate, a little fatter, but penetration did funny things to his body, turning to goo on the heated spire of Rhys' cock just as he always did.

Sometimes, Guy wondered if he had the same effect on the hawk as Rhys had on him. But they'd have to talk about that when they weren't wrapped up in the heat of the moment, panting heavily, letting every thrust roll through him. He tightened his grip around Rhys' hips and thrust back up against him with all the quivering leverage he had left in his body.

For it was not all about the Harris hawk thrusting, after all, but what his body could give back to him too in terms of pleasure. Every stroke of the hawk's dick had him quivering, tongue lolling from his mouth, yet Rhys would have been hard-pressed indeed to find anyone more beautiful than the fox in that moment.

And that was just why he kept going, working them both closer and closer to their highs. There was nothing else there, only the pursuit of pleasure, and they hunted it down together: two predator species, even though one was of the land and the other of the sky. It was a good analogy, even though it had been a long time since Rhys' body had been light enough to fly, though that was just something a lot of avian anthros had to deal with.

"Unff… Getting closer, foxie…"

Rhys gave him warning as he sped up, his hips rising to a sharp slap against Guy's buttocks. Yet the fox was there to bear through every stroke, even as his throat hitched and twitched, Adam's apple bobbing in an overdue gulp of saliva.

For the bird knew his boyfriend was even closer than he was, giving it all he had, though focusing increasingly on the fox's shaft. The mostly hard length throbbed furtively within the clasp of his palm and fingers as he worked him over and the fox, squirming all the while, had nowhere to go other than into the arms of orgasm itself.

He howled under Rhys, every stroke bringing him to a flourish of pleasure that built and built, his cock dripping and spurting all over his lower abdomen, though Guy had never been one for a massive cum shot, no. That didn't matter, not as Rhys sped up again, catching his breath the best he could and hammering into the fox's tight, clenching tail hole in a series of near manic, overpowering thrusts.

Yet that was the moment and Guy licked his lips as the hawk slammed in ruthlessly. It was the point at which those heavy, short strokes came into their own, even if Guy would be ever so slightly sore the next day.

That was all part of coming together in that way and neither would change it for the world as, finally, Rhys screeched and let his hips judder all the way up to the fox, releasing his load.

For a moment, the world stood still, the stars all that could bear witness to the swirling frenzy of need tangled between them. Rhys pressed in as deep as he could go and stayed there, allowing the twitch and pull of Guy's tail hole to massage him, even if there was no specific rhythm to it. It was just what they needed, both dragging in raw, raking breaths, Guy's cum lightly cooling on his belly as his cock softened a little more, draping itself against his lower abdomen.

The bird's shaft, however, remained achingly hard as he stayed deep, sending hot spurt after spurt into the fox's tail hole. He wanted more, desperate for it, but would have to linger there, savouring every throb.

Of course, there could be plenty more to come later, though they had to take their time, have their patience. They would always, after all, have one another there.

Guy rubbed his paws over his face, blindly reaching up for his partner. The avian's fingers clasped his, holding him fast, and the hawk withdrew slightly, so he could more easily fold forward over his partner's body. The fox's legs slumped to the ground, still spread, and he wrapped his arms around Rhys, breathing in his scent as he buried his nose in the crook of the hawk's neck.

Together, wherever they were, would be home to them. Clad in the simple solitude of the wilderness, lips and beak met in a soft, passionate kiss.

The night was young and they had nowhere to be.

Convention Romp

He was in Mike's arms before he knew it, the edges of his mind fuzzy with alcohol, even though he was very much on board with what was happening. The fursuiter walked ahead of him, clutching his hand tightly, though Mike's fursuit was a more form-fitting dragon one, showing his natural shape while enhancing his shoulders and the muscle of his legs. Who wouldn't want to look even better as their fursona at a furry convention, after all, than they did in real life? It was all about the fantasy, after all.

Still, Tom blushed as they tumbled into the bedroom together, locking the door, though it was Tom who had to fumble to put the chain in place, fingers clumsy at such a late hour. Or early, depending on how one looked at it, the parties still in full swing through several rooms and the dance floor itself, the main foyer crowded with furs all looking to meet up. But all he wanted as he loosened his belt, blushing heavily, was Mike on top of him, the dragon-fur growling playfully.

"Hey, you don't need me to take the suit off, do you?"

Tom blinked.

"What?"

He was already back on the bed, his shirt pulled up to expose his lower stomach, the blue of his underwear showing through where his jeans had loosened. But Mike was over him, still in suit, working his fingers around his crotch as if…

"No…"

Tom had to do it for him in the end, laughing aloud. It didn't seem real, none of it – Mike had never told him that he had a murrsuit! It hadn't even looked anything like what he'd expected one of those to look like, a blended in panel that looked like a dragon's plate scales (even if it was all well-trimmed and groomed fake fur) coming away to reveal the zip beneath. It was that zip that could be pulled down by Tom's fingers, though he gave it a quick go with his teeth, the hotel room familiar and yet strange around him.

"Oh, god..."

Revealing the bulge of Mike's cock through his underwear, the zip allowing it, Tom groaned, pressing his face to it, inhaling deeply. Sure, there was a deeper kind of musk in there, but that was no matter to him, for his temporary partner's cock would be out in due course. It was awkward, the hidden zipper not large enough for Tom to get his hand in there, but it had to work, even if that liaison had not been something that they'd been expecting.

They'd work it out. Somehow. Pulling Mike's underwear down, his cock sprung free, on show and heady, though the hand on Tom's head drew him in. His lips parted, taking the "dragon's" cock deep into the back of his mouth, swallowing around it, though the room swayed around him, his grip on the moment weakening.

Somehow... It felt like he was really sucking off a dragon, as if he could really take Mike as a dragon. He shivered, pushing his jeans down, wriggling them past his hips, his own shaft pushing out on show, though the waistband of his underwear popped down in front of his balls, keeping those hidden. For the moment, maybe that was the best way of it, skin prickling with heat, sweat trickling down between his shoulder blades.

He groaned around Mike's shaft, swirling his tongue around, the flesh of the dragon's uncut length pushing over his tongue. It was smooth, so fleshy, allowing him to push his tongue around the head, even if he wanted to bob his head, to suck harder, to give Mike as much pleasure as possible. Amidst the musk, there was a thicker taste from a drop of pre-cum but, alas, human beings did not produce as much cum as dragons in fantasy and other furry beings, though he could still imagine.

Tom's cock throbbed. He was a canine fur, a German Shepherd – though he didn't feel big and bold before Mike. Even the sway of the dragon's tail tipped him back and forth lightly, adding to the moment, the weight of it balancing him, making it seem like he was a dragon, the fun in the moment most potent with a zipper on the suit both up and down at the same time. Mike groaned, head tipping back, though his words were lost in his lust as he thrust and ground.

"Fuck... Yes..."

Their lust rebounded, shared between the two of them as Tom sucked him down, losing himself in that moment. Right then and there, he was not really at a furry convention, but off in some fantasy world with the guy he'd been talking to for months, the dragon of his dreams, giving him the blowjob of his life and then some. That was all he had to think about, all that he had to lust for, as he groaned aloud, cock in one hand and the other resting on the fur of Mike's thigh.

"Ah... Hell, Tom, that feels so good..."

Alas, that cock withdrew from his lips, leaving Mike leaning after it, eyes wide and plaintive. He could not see the dragon fur's expression, but it would have to be as it was, Mike gently but firmly drawing him upright as he stood there. A dragon's paws in fursuit were not as dextrous as the hands of a man without, but there was no question as to whether they were more erotic or not. Tom shivered, Mike's paws stroking all over, though it was down to Tom to undress himself fully, revealing his pale-skinned flesh in all its glory.

The body, however, was not the appeal as Mike closed his paw around Tom's cock, pumping and stroking, teasing with the alluring stroke of fur. It was a new sensation, something different, something that had him weak at the knees as he sat on the edge of the bed, spreading his legs, letting the dragon do all that he wanted with him. He lay back, stretching his arms out over his head, letting Mike hitch his legs up, the hardness of his cock resting against his belly while the dragon's pressed to the tightness of his anal ring.

"Let me know how slow I need to go..."

He groaned, head spinning. The coolness of the lubrication splashed over Mike's shaft, though was not neatly placed, the dragon not caring too much about smearing it all over. With what they had in mind, it would surely get to where it needed to go.

Tom tensed, striving to relax, his shoulder blades digging into the bed, trying to arch, though Mike already had one leg hitched up around his waist. The dragon loomed over him, dominating his line of vision, and if he had been in any other position Tom would have swooned. Oh, to be under a real dragon, submitting like that... It would have been his greatest dream and biggest fantasy, but some things had to be settled with in fursuit, something that he hardly believed he was getting to do.

And Mike too. He would get to know him more later. There would be more there for the two of them, though one night of passion would only be the beginning.

That shaft begged for entry, pushing in, stretching him open, though neither of them were virgins. They knew what to do, but it felt like the first time all over again to Tom as his backside was penetrated, gasping aloud, clutching at Mike as if he was the only thing rooting him in place. Mike held him tightly, though the fur was too warm, the scent of fresh sweat filling the air, even though it would all be worth it, they were both sure.

He groaned deep in the back of his throat, the sense of being full spreading through him. His backside tried to squeeze down against his will, though all he needed to do was relax, to take the slow, empowering thrusts of the dragon as he filled him, again and again. Locking eyes with him through the mesh viewing tear ducts of the suit, Mike growled playfully, wiggling his hips just to make it look like he was swishing his tail. Little things like that added to the illusion that he was a dragon, not just one wearing a suit.

But Tom wanted more, panting, holding his shaft, squeezing lightly, though the dragon's cock pushed over a part of his backdoor entrance that made his dick pulse pre-cum all the same. He didn't truly need his own dick to be fully hard, not as he softened around that cock, allowing Mike to speed up his thrusts, filling him repeatedly, stroke after stroke hitting home as if the two of them were supposed to be together.

Maybe they could have been more cautious, maybe it was the heat of the moment. But putting on a condom simply had not factored at a time like that. They'd discuss it in the morning, over a buffet breakfast with shy smiles and hot cheeks, but that would have to wait a while yet. They had better things to worry about imminently, moans rising, hips bucking, even Tom trying to press up from his position on the bed. He had a little leverage, squeezing his legs around the dragons' hips and waist, holding onto him.

The strain of his pucker was rampant, however, something that he could not take his mind from – not that he would have wanted to. The dragon above him huffed and panted, just like what he imagined a real one sounded like, bearing into him with short, needy thrusts. It was not for either of them, after all, to deny themselves the needs of the body, sheets rumpling under Tom's back as he twisted, grasping at all that he could.

Nothing locked him down as his head spun, body twisting, panting, heaving, hand closed around his shaft. Orgasm overtook him without his mind catching up with what was happening, cum painting his lower stomach, dribbling and drooling, spurting forth as if his body was trying to prove a visual point. As much as he panted and moaned, however, the sticking point of it all was the climax of the dragon before him, wings lifting above his back as he thrust, needing more, his tight hole clenching around Mike's shaft as if it was the only thing left that he could do.

Mike, finally, cried out too as orgasm took him, for neither of them fully felt in control as he drove in hard and fast, thrusting through climax. Clinging to him, Tom panted and moaned, back arching, trying to get even more of his partner's cock into him, tightening up in the aftermath, even though he was too sensitive, truly, to be penetrated.

But he would bear through every last second of it as Mike collapsed over him with a low, throaty moan, holding him tightly, the fur too hot, too clinging, but neither of them caring one bit about that. They were there in the afterglow for each other, even if they still had to understand and learn about one another, panting and heaving, striving to catch their breath. There would be plenty of time for that.

Like with so much, there was no rush left when they had plenty of time to spend with each other, even beyond the con itself. And who knew that such things could come of a furry convention, really?

Tom sighed happily, his backside tightening around Mike's length, even as it softened. The dragon nuzzled him as if they were kissing, a giggle on Tom's lips, kissing back, imagining that there was a long, slender tongue winding around his. The start of something new could not have come at a better time for either of them.

And the start of that something could only come from a convention romp with someone who meant so much to him.

The Next Chapter

"So, this is it then, is it?"

Salem smiled, the black rabbit's ears standing tall, no malice in his tone. He was an older student, by a little, in his late twenties, though his light, slight figure gave the impression that he was younger than he was. He leaned back on the wall, looking out across the university grounds, although things were already much quieter.

It was the last day of the student accommodation halls being filled, at least for those studying during the regular semesters, ending in early Summer and starting in the Autumn. So late at night, most of the students had already left and the campus was left eerily quiet, the old, stone buildings towering solemnly. The ground was not level throughout the campus and the spot he'd chosen, up on a wall, looked down over a good portion of the old university. The coniferous trees blocked the newer parts of the campus from view.

That suited him. He didn't need to think of what was ahead, for there was going to be an awful lot of that going forward and it was not as if it had not been drilled into him over the last year of his degree. Even though he should have been focusing on his degree and his studies, it had loomed there regardless, dauntingly ahead. But he wanted to consider what had been and delve into it, uncovering fresh truths that had been in plain sight all the time.

Salem smiled. He had a weird way of thinking – or so his parents had said. The bunny had got along well with others at the Northern university, although his parents had not quite meshed well with him.

Night had fallen and the streetlamps were on, illuminating parts of the university grounds while some areas were still cast into darkness. A laugh echoed across the campus, hollow and echoing, though Salem couldn't tell just where it had come from. There were barely any around and that was fine by him.

Yet Salem was a graduate and, for the rabbit, there was no reason for him to stay around the university, other than nostalgia. He'd graduated from his undergraduate degree around a month ago and he wasn't moving on into a master's degree, purely as the cost was too steep. It was time to move on, into the world of work, though Salem was not at all sure how long his savings would last or how swiftly he was going to be able to find his first step into real work. Mostly likely for him, he'd end up with a job he could take to get by for a little while, waiting sensibly for his better move into a career working with something historical. On that side, Salem didn't want to be too rigid in his path.

Yet there was nothing left for him at the university. Besides Baxter, of course, the moderately built husky with a softness around his middle. They'd been close during their time studying at the university, in the old buildings with all their quirks, but what the rabbit had thought was a budding relationship between them had not quite come to fruition as he'd thought. There'd been so many late nights talking between him and the husky, sitting up, spilling all their secrets. There'd even been outings that may as well have been dates, for others assumed they were together, making a "cute couple."

He wasn't sure if he wanted to be with Baxter, however. There was a spark there, but what did it mean when they were, most likely, going to be off living elsewhere after university? Baxter was supposed to be heading back down south to the Gloucester area or something like that, though the husky hadn't quite decided yet. Salem didn't have a direction in his life, so he was flexible – but to follow the canine south just seemed insane. He wasn't that kind of guy, to throw it all to the wind and risk it all. Especially when all that was between them, so far, was a friendship.

"Fancy seeing you here."

The rabbit's ears pricked and his back stiffened, a chill spiking down his spine. Oh, how had he missed his pawsteps? The husky trod heavily and yet Salem had been so deep in his own thoughts that he had not caught on to the canine approaching in the slightest.

He tried to ignore how his heart skipped a beat, his stomach churning pleasantly, warmly. It meant more than the bunny was, so far, willing to admit to.

Yet time was running out and Salem knew it too as he turned to the husky, taking in his soft, grey fur, a hint of blue streaked through his short, fluffed up hair. He wasn't sure whether Baxter had styled it that day, though the bunny still thought it looked good. He would always think Baxter looked good, regardless of what he was wearing or how he was trying out a new style.

But that was just one of the many reasons he was as quietly, softly infatuated with the husky was he was, even if nothing had come to light there. He smiled lightly but tried not to let his smile wobble.

It's okay, he told himself. *You'll stay in touch. It doesn't need to be any more than that, that's all this is. Be glad he's your friend.*

"Yeah," Salem said at last. "Yeah, I just wanted to see everything, before I headed off from the accommodation."

"Didn't you have it for another week or two?" Baxter said with a smile, hopping up casually on to the wall next to the bunny. "Lucky. Running off after all this... It seems weird. Like we're not actually ready for it."

"I get that," Salem said in a rush of exhaled breath. "It's... It's a lot. It's a big change. But we've got to do it. I know you'll only have exciting things ahead."

"Yeah!" Baxter barked, the sharp sound echoing through the night air. "I got two job interviews set up already, I'm nervous... Got to try though, haven't I?"

He squirmed and Salem shifted in closer to him, stealing a touch of warmth from the canine's body. He was going to miss that.

"I really hope you get one of them, whatever's best for you," the rabbit said. "Do you need any help preparing? I don't think the careers thing here was all that good."

"Heh..." Baxter chuckled, shifting and rubbing the back of his neck. "Yeah, I'd love the help, thanks. They told me to put my CV in a weird format, on pink paper... Said it'd stand out? Don't they know all that stuff is digital these days?"

Salem winced, though enjoyed the closeness of the dog all the same.

"Yeah, that's ridiculous," he muttered. "Maybe it would have worked, twenty...thirty years ago. It's so different now."

"Yep, that's right."

They sat there in companionable silence for a few long moments, not sure whether for seconds or minutes. They'd always been good at that, the quiet between them, and Salem liked how comfortable it was. He'd never felt that comfortable with someone else.

"So, are you staying here for a bit?"

Baxter broke the quiet, though Salem could not help but notice his paw on the stone wall between them. It was so close, yet the bunny didn't dare move. Could it be an accident?

And what if it wasn't? What good would that do them, after everything? They were going their separate ways, at least in physical location.

"I think so," Salem said quietly, not wanting to spoil the moment. "But there's more work down south too. I don't know what I want to do yet, but maybe I'll get lucky. There're some places looking for graduates at this time of year, so I want to see how job searching for something actually in my field goes first. Before I settle for an interim job or whatever."

"I know you'll make it," the husky said, turning to look at him, though the rabbit still kept his eyes fixed forward, shivering in place. "It's going to be okay, I just know it. You always do whatever you set your mind to."

The rabbit laughed before he could stop himself.

"No, I don't."

The words left him too quickly and Salem regretted them immediately. The canine's attention locked on to him and Salem tried to play it off as a passing comment, not anything of any real significance. He didn't want to make a big deal of it, not even then.

"Hm… What's up with that?" Baxter probed lightly. "Did you forget to do something? Maybe we still have time to do it, you know… Before we have to leave?"

Salem's heart hammered. No, no… Oh, no, he couldn't do that. He couldn't say it, couldn't do it. It was too late for anything like that, they'd missed their chance. And he didn't even know if Baxter felt at all the same way.

Hell, the rabbit didn't even know how he felt.

Maybe that was why he did it.

Salem hadn't had anything to drink, so he couldn't blame the alcohol as he turned to face the husky. His muzzle turned slowly, very slowly, giving

Baxter ample opportunity to put space between them again. It could have been easy to play off, as if it had not happened at all, the two of them friends and nothing more than that.

Yet the husky did not squirm away and seemed to be holding his breath too as the bunny stared into his eyes, drinking in the blue pools. He wanted to lose himself in those eyes, even though prolonged eye contact was hard for him. There were even flecks of green and brown in there too, but not all that many. Salem had to look really hard for them.

Baxter had stood by him even when a group had tried to bully him. Thankfully, with how things were at universities those days, it hadn't come to all that much, which was a lot more than could be said for how others treated Salem way back in school. Still, having the husky on his side had meant a lot to him, as if the canine had known, intrinsically, just what he'd needed without even having to ask for it.

He needed that. He wanted that. More than having someone in his corner, but someone who cared so deeply for him that he never even had to question what was going on, sensing little things without needing to have it all stated explicitly.

"Salem?"

The husky breathed his name, breath tickling the bunny's lips. They were close, too close, and neither moved away.

So, Salem did it. He did what he perhaps should have done a long time ago and closed the distance between them, sealing his lips in a gentle, breathy kiss against the husky's own. It was where he needed to be and tension eased from the roll of his shoulders, his small tail lifting and twitching.

For a moment, no one did any more than that. And then everything slotted neatly, breathlessly, into place, as if the very air they shared between their mouths had something more potent altogether in it. Baxter's paws came up around him, one folding sweetly into the curve of the bunny's lower back to pull him off the wall while the other clung to his arm. There was a desperate bite to the husky's fingers, digging in faintly, though Salem was comfortable with it.

He wanted to be held and hungrily pulled close like that, letting out a muffled groan into the kiss. It might have been a sob or a cry that rose from a more carnal part of his psyche, although the bunny didn't care.

It all came through, at least for them, in the next chapter.

With nothing else around them in the dead of the night, the kiss deepened, opening a door to something they hadn't been clear enough with one another about. His lips parted against the husky's as they tasted one another, their tongues flicking and curling inside their mouths, sweeping up against each other. It was a clumsy sort of kiss, but a kiss like that was one full of promise.

There was so much ahead and they would work it out. The moment was about them, however, and the connection that should have been paid due attention much, much earlier.

Salem's paws shakily rested on the husky's chest, although he didn't want to push him away. He just didn't know what it was he was supposed to be doing to draw him closer, to meld his essence with that of Baxter's, beautifully losing himself.

They broke the kiss, panting, only to crush their lips back together more fervently. Tilting their heads the other direction, Salem managed to find the boldness to cup the husky's cheek, his fingers folding nicely up the line of his jaw. It was as if they were meant to fit together.

"Baxter... I..."

Salem tried to find words, though his lips barely left the husky's as his head spun pleasantly. The husky, however, was quick to quiet him. A smile twitched at his lips as he turned Salem's head gently, only enough so he could kiss him on the side of his short muzzle, lips tickling the bunny's twitching nose.

"It's okay, it's okay," he whispered, hardly raising his voice at all. "We're here now, it's okay... Salem, I'm sorry, we should have... I should have..."

Yet Baxter struggled with words, his tail wagging. Salem kissed him again, a chaste kiss that time even though his lips were slightly parted still.

Salem exhaled, ears twitching.

"Please, come with me," Salem said. "Back to mine. We need to...talk."

They weren't, however, going to do much talking that night, even if they found a way to extend Salem's accommodation stay there, just by a couple of weeks. Their directions did not have to be different, even then, but the morning and daylight hours would bring further revelations there.

Paw in paw, they stumbled their way back to Salem's small flat, even if it was more than enough for a student. Tumbling up the stairs, somehow, they laughed and scrambled, intent only on getting in and through the door.

They could have talked, but he enjoyed the moment for what it was, fumbling with one another's clothes and, too quickly, undressing each other. They'd seen each other in various stages of undress before – but not all the way.

"I... You know..."

Salem paused the husky before he got his underwear off, jeans already pooling around the rabbit's ankles. Of course, Baxter knew he had undergone bottom surgery before attending university, which was one of the reasons why he was attending as a mature student and not fresh out of college, but he hadn't seen it. The transgender rabbit was merely grateful for being able to live his life as himself and in the exact way he wanted. His body was his to do with as he willed – and it seemed Baxter didn't mind that either.

"It's okay, seriously, don't think about that," Baxter said, rushing over his words. "Come on…"

The husky whimpered as he helped the rabbit out of his underwear, freeing a half-hard shaft. It didn't often get hard enough for penetration, not without a little help, though that didn't bother the rabbit all that much. His sex drive had differed over different hormone therapies. But before uncovering his true self, he honestly had even wondered if he was asexual, for he just didn't have that kind of interest.

It took understanding himself to feel attraction, however, and he was glad that had all come through. Even if his body was not quite as he would have wanted it to be born: he had come a lot further than many had said he was ever going to be able to. He could not have a sheath around the base of his shaft, but it was large enough for him at four inches, the head more sensitive than any other part. A pair of small balls had been made below, while he did not think of the sex he'd been born with for anything more than medical needs.

It wasn't for him. It had never been for him. So, he put it from his mind, his cock aching as the tip tingled. Even the brush of the husky's paw over the head, thumbing it, had him rocking his hips, grinding forward with lust pooling at his core.

"Mmm…"

The husky hummed happily, nipping and nibbling at the rabbit's neck. Salem moaned and leaned into the canine's touch, shivering all over. Electric shocks of pleasure ached through him and he whimpered lightly, trying not to let too much roll through him all at once.

It was to be savoured, at the very least. There didn't have to be a rush, not when they were there to explore and enjoy each other's bodies to the best of their abilities.

"Ah… Oh, that feels…" Salem grunted, nose twitching. "Mm, can you come up on the bed with me? Please?"

"Of course," Baxter moaned as the rabbit's paws found his hips, fingers sliding down towards his crotch. "Ah… Yes…"

The husky still had his boxers on, though they didn't hide anything. Even though Salem was comfortable, increasingly so with every passing minute, with Baxter running his paws over his body, he really wanted to see what Baxter had to offer. There was a softness to the husky's body that he rather liked, enjoying the comfort and warmth.

Yet his shaft was larger than the bunny's and throbbed into Salem's eager touch. It was of a size where he couldn't close his fingers all the way around – though, to be fair, the rabbit wasn't trying all that hard to.

"Mmm… Oh," he murmured, a little surprised by what he found. "I forgot you'd have a sheath, heh…"

"Oh, yeah," Baxter moaned, his boxers sliding all the way down, leaving both of them perfectly nude, but for their fur. "Yeah… It kind of gets a bit tight on my length sometimes. But it's…mmm…yeah…"

The husky wasn't thinking clearly enough to get all his words out as he wanted. He panted heavily, a flexible length of pink tongue spilling from his maw. They kissed, the bunny straddling the husky's hips, though it took his legs a little more to spread around them. Baxter was more broadly built than Salem and the bunny groaned into his mouth, heart pounding.

It was better when they had that physical closeness between them, kissing deeply and languidly exploring one another's muzzles. The canine kissed him almost desperately, every lap of his tongue seeming to hit all the right spots. Or maybe the moment was simply that right for them both that everything came together sweetly, only the sounds of the street outside and the quiet nighttime city to keep them company.

There, they could relax into each other and Salem exhaled hotly, grinding his semi-hard shaft against the husky's. It was strange to push and roll his hips against someone else like that and he worried, for a moment, that his inexperience showed. Well, not technically inexperience, for he just hadn't been with anyone in over a year. Yet he'd wanted to make sure everything was right, that he wasn't just going about having sex for the sake of it.

It had been worth it, in the end, for him to wait for Baxter, the husky's cock dribbling pre-cum. His shaft could not do that, but that was okay as far as he was concerned: it could be a little messy. And he didn't have the concern of getting a hard-on in public (that would have been surprising!) to worry about either.

He had all the best parts for himself, his body thrumming with delight as ecstasy rolled through him.

The husky groaned, breaking the kiss to pull back slightly, his tail wagging.

He was about to say something, although Salem didn't know what either of them could say that their bodies could not in a moment like that. He moaned lightly, licking his lips, though the bunny had his fingers around the dog's cock, stroking up and down.

Baxter humped into Salem's paw, though their cocks still bumped against one another, sliding back and forth. It was such a carnal motion, with the bunny on top, and he followed the will of his body, thrusting and grinding as if nothing else mattered.

It was the headiness of lust, tangled with something more, something deeper, between them that kept them going. There was nothing to hold the bunny and the husky back as Baxter grunted and let out a tiny growl, the pre-cum dribbling down his length and allowing Salem's paw to slide back and forth more easily. They kissed more tenderly, taking things at a slower pace and not minding at all the exchange of saliva between them. It was warm and slick and made Salem want to press into the husky even more.

Salem's eyelids fluttered, breaking the kiss so he could explore Baxter a little. As hard as it was to pull his cock away from the husky's, where they had been grinding while he'd used his paw on the dog's cock too, he wanted to taste him too. There was something simply instinctual about it, holding the tenderest part of another guy in his mouth, and he wouldn't deny himself that.

So, he slid down, even if it put his own crotch at a distance from the husky, only thinking of their shared experience. His lips trailed a path down the husky's body and over his cock, kissing the pulsing length softly and sweetly.

A groan from the canine encouraged him on and he panted lightly, his tail twitching. A bunny's tail was too small to really show anything in such a position, though Salem was not to know the dog's eyes were on him, raking adoringly over his form. There was a hunger in those eyes too, but he wanted to enjoy every moment, letting himself sink deeper and deeper.

Baxter was love itself, at least to him. But he could linger there, lusting over the moment, licking his lips, rocking his own hips as his need ached deep inside. One day, he'd say those three not so little words to Baxter and everything would change.

For the better. Until then, they were both in it solely to enjoy the ride, no more and no less than that.

Salem's lips parted curiously over the head of the husky's cock, catching Baxter's murmur to him. Yet he wanted to enjoy the moment even more, suckling it inside and holding the dog's cock up a little, so it was at a better angle for him to please. The husky whimpered and rocked his hips up, so Salem kept going, stretching his lips wider around his shaft and suckling it as deep into his mouth as he could.

"Ohhhh, oh, that feels good… Ah, Salem…" The husky moaned. "That's amazing, I love it. Your mouth feels so good. But I want to feel…even more of you."

"Mmph?"

Salem squinted up the length of the husky's body, although it was difficult for him to see the canine's muzzle when he was in such a position. His muzzle slid up and down the length of Baxter's shaft, cradling the base as it plumped up ever so slightly. That was the dog's knot, although it would not be sinking into the rabbit that night.

Another time for that. There would be plenty of time and Salem's tongue pressed teasingly up to the underside of the canine's shaft, savouring every inch of him. There was a slickness on his tongue from the husky's pre-cum that sent an aching thrum through his body, yet it was the smooth length of cock that captivated him. The tip, tapered, almost bounced off his tongue when he came up to it, though Salem was too caught up in adoring Baxter's shaft to stay up there for too long.

He groaned around the husky and turned his muzzle back and forth slightly, rotating a small amount around Baxter's cock, just to find what suited them both. His tongue pressed out over his lower lip as he sank all the way down, exploring just how much of Baxter's length he could take, though it was difficult as the tip ground into the back of his throat. The bunny's muzzle was shorter than the husky's, after all, and he swallowed around him, ignoring the glisten of moisture in the corners of his eyes.

The strain was worth it, of course. He lusted for it and lost himself there, savouring Baxter. Yet the husky's paws were not idle either as Salem bobbed his head up and down, lavishing as much attention on him as he felt was possible to do. Baxter's fingers smoothed down the rabbit's ears and between them, scratching and teasing, even working their way down to the back of Salem's neck.

It was all Salem could do to focus, yet he didn't want to be there forever. Not really, not when there was so much more of the husky to enjoy, but it was hard to pick what he wanted to do at any given time.

"Ah, please… Salem," Baxter coaxed him, gently raising the rabbit's head from his head, the tip springing wetly free of Salem's lips. "Come up here. I want you. Can we?"

It was a good thing the canine was about to take charge of picking, in that case, but it would only bring them closer together. The rabbit knelt over the husky's hips again as he directed Baxter to fish out the lube from the drawer of the bedside table. It only took a few moments for the husky to help Salem lube up his tail hole, the tight pucker begging attention.

From there, it was all up to Salem just how quickly he took things as he slowly sat down on Baxter's length. His backside strained deliciously around the husky's cock as he took it, bit by bit, taking his time despite the lube.

Baxter panted, clasping his paw, their fingers interlinked as if he never again wanted to let go. Their eyes met as he rocked his hips, slowly riding the husky's cock as his ass was, very pleasantly, stretched open around his girth.

"Ah... Baxter... I wish I'd said something sooner," Salem groaned, so quietly it was a wonder the husky even heard him at all. "Thank you... Let's... We'll make something work."

And they would. Because it was the two of them, both in it together. They needed nothing more than that, at their stage in life, the husky letting the rabbit take the lead as much as he liked, guiding the pace. Yet Baxter didn't need to be idle as he took Salem's smaller shaft in his paw, a cheeky glint in his eye.

"Tell me what feels good, hon," the husky grunted, licking his lips. "I'd do anything for you."

Salem nodded and gently guided the husky in stroking his cock. It was not a shaft that could be pleased more simply – but it still felt good to have it rubbed up and down too, it was not as if that was a bad thing in the slightest. The head was the most sensitive and there were certain actions, like pressing back up towards the tip, that felt the best.

It was one way to achieve orgasm also that he liked, panting more heavily like he was a canine himself, Salem's chest heaving. The rabbit grunted and folded his ears back, need rising, though he couldn't bear to close his eyes.

He wanted to take in everything, so he memorised every single moment. From the shuddering rise of the husky's chest to how his tail flicked, curled up and still twitching back between Baxter's legs. The light scent of sex and sweat hung in the air, yet the moment was all they needed it to be, grunting headily and taking their pleasure.

It was not about orgasm but the journey to it. The rabbit rocked his hips more urgently, grinding down on to the husky's shaft, wanting more, aching for it. Yet Baxter was there to catch him as his need rose and rose, even though the canine's knot was growing even more.

Baxter, however, squeezed it in his paw, his fingers pinching around it, keeping it out of Salem's tail hole. It would have been too much of a stretch the first time, with how thick around it was, and it was not as if it had been sunk into the bunny's anal passage before inflating to its full girth.

They climaxed together, lust tightening inside them, pleasure coming to a beautiful crescendo. Actually, it was Baxter who got off first, the tight clench and pull of the bunny's tail hole simply too much for him as he ejaculated, losing control and sending long, hot spurts of cum into his partner. The amount of his seed was not the point, however, not as the closeness and intimacy between them thrummed, the bunny thrusting into the husky's paw.

And Baxter, with the tension crackling beautifully between them, brought the rabbit off only a few moments later. The pressure on his most sensitive of areas was too much and Salem let out a cry, thrusting rampantly into his paw. The jerk of his hips was not to be controlled and he groaned open-mouthed, letting it roll through him. There was no ejaculation from the rabbit, of course, but it was just as good, clenching with both his passages while lust coursed through him, pulse after devout pulse.

Until he came down and collapsed on the husky's chest, his chin propped up below Baxter's chin, grunting lightly. He couldn't get out any words, lips parted, his chest lightly damp with sweat as he squirmed there, trying to get comfortable. The dog's cock was still inside him, softening slowly, yet the knot remained engorged – thankfully outside his tail hole, that time.

Their eyes met and Salem giggled, the heat of a blush rising from his cheeks. No words needed to be shared, not as he squeezed the canine's paw, holding him close even then.

It was their next chapter, together. It was all up to them just how things changed, what they did, where they took things – and neither could be happier for that.

Things could have been very different if they hadn't made their feelings known that night. Yet a world of possibilities stretched out before them, once they were ready to write their next chapter.

Together, that was exactly what Baxter and Salem would do.

A Little Rougher

"Unff…"

"Oh, you can do better than that, Matheo," the hyena said, standing over the red fox with a smirk. "Come on. Try to moan for me. You were so loud before, weren't you? But you're not so noisy with a cute little ball gag stuffed into your maw."

The fox, Matheo, shuddered and shook his head, though he was quite happy where he was. Bound on his back on the bed, so his boyfriend had full access to every part of him, including his throbbing member, there was nothing he could do to protect himself. His fur was matted between the legs and under his arms where he had sweated, though not all anthros sweated in that manner. It depended on them as individuals and the musky taint of fox lingered in the air of the bedroom.

It had been a long week, although that wasn't something Matheo had to think about anymore. That was why he was there, bound on the bed as he was. Tian, as he always did, saw he'd been struggling – and took away all that doubt and frustration from him in the blink of an eye. If he was bound and submissive, he didn't have to think too hard and he didn't have to concern himself with anything other than pleasing his "master."

It was perfect.

Tian smiled more gently when he turned away from the fox, taking a moment for himself. Dominating could be tiring, yet it was what his partner needed – and he was there to take care of Matheo too. It was not all about him, which was the mistake some dominants made when they were playing out a scene, or even in a deeper relationship dynamic.

Coming from Africa after being in a long-distance relationship with Matheo in England, the hyena would be forever glad he'd found the fox. His chest was narrow and slender with little muscle definition there, but that was only because he was on the slimmer side. Everything about him was light and lithe, almost delicate, while Tian was a little shorter than him and of a stockier build.

Tian ran his fingers back through his short tuft of hair, which ruffed up around his head and the back of his neck as if it was reminiscent of a more mane-like feature, still in the hyena fashion. Yet when he turned back to Matheo, he had a butt plug in his paws.

"Squeeze the ball to stop anytime," Tian said firmly, making eye contact with the fox as he referred to the squeaky ball the fox held in his paw. "Do you understand? Nod if you understand."

Although it took a great effort of will for Matheo to satisfy that need, his body aching deliciously, he managed to nod, tipping his chin down towards his chest, twice. The sheets rumpled a little under him, but that was only the start of tiny discomforts he was set to endure.

Even in the familiar bedroom, a place of safety and sanctuary, it felt amazing. It was good to have him there, to slip away, as if everything was different simply because they had taken on their preferred roles in the bedroom.

He relaxed back, whimpering, as Tian toyed with him. With a slick coat of lubrication, just to make it easier, the butt plug teased up against his backside, the rounded, smooth tip pressed into his tail hole.

"Oof..."

He moaned around the gag in his mouth, pushing his tongue against the smooth, silicone surface of the ball there. The red fox could dig his teeth into it if needed, yet there was a part of him that didn't want to mark it in any way. He loved to keep everything his partner and he owned as pristine as possible, even if that was not always possible.

"Relax, pet."

The fox tried to. He rolled his hips forward, yet there was only so far he could go. His arms and legs were spread a little, just enough so that Tian could get under his rump to his tail hole, though there was a small, soft pillow propped under the fox's ass too. It was the little things that made a scene work, so they didn't have to deal with any spots of awkwardness in the moment.

That, however, was Tian's domain, not Matheo's. The fox moaned longingly around the gag as the butt plug eased deeper and deeper, though he had failed to notice what Tian had tucked into the palm of his paw.

For, as soon as the entire, moderately sized plug was buried in his rump, the hyena smirked. Matheo flinched, but not in a bad way. He knew something was coming and his muscles tensed, shoulder pushing back a little more. Despite understanding he was quite safe there, he twitched his fingers around the small, squeaky ball in the palm of his own paw, fingers curled around it to make sure he didn't drop it. If he dropped it, that counted as a safe word too – as well as squeezing it to make it squeak, as Tian had already directed him.

A safe scene was a good scene: even if things were a little rougher.

The fox groaned, the plug shifting inside him. That didn't feel quite right, although it felt good too. His ass clenched, squeezing around it, and he tried to lick his lips, his tongue coming up against the gag once again.

Tian laughed softly, though not meanly.

"Can you feel that? It's going to get bigger, so much bigger…"

The fox whined, blinking down at his body. He couldn't see what was inside him, of course not, but he felt the plug growing larger and larger inside him with every squeeze of the hyena's paw. Tian pumped up the inflatable butt plug, bearing it up against his prostate as the fox squirmed deliciously.

It was a lot and there was surely no way he would have been able to take a plug like that size, without a lot more preparation, if it had all had to squeeze by his anal ring. His ass tightened, despite knowing he had to allow some space for the plug to grow, yet the fox simply couldn't help himself.

It felt too good to stop. His body quivered, fingers twitching, toes curling. Everything heightened, sensation crawling across his skin, his chest rising and falling more sharply as he dragged in needy pants through his nostrils. Matheo would have been panting through an open maw if he'd had the chance, yet that was not to be so.

The hyena loomed above him, even though he was bending forward. Still, Tian cut an imposing figure, regardless of the position he was in. The hyena's tail twitched lightly and a smirk tugged playfully at his lips as he squeezed the small, attached bulb of the butt plug, which was what allowed it to inflate. If he wanted to deflate and shrink it, all Tian would need to do would be to press the button in on the end of the bulb, allowing the air to escape.

Under the hyena, Matheo moaned and rolled his hips up, the ropes allowing him some freedom of motion. The mere inches he was allowed to shift gave him a false sense of being able to free himself, although it was not as if the fox wanted to be free. He needed to struggle, if only a little, so he knew he was safe there, that he was secure under Tian's strong paw.

"Breathe, little fox."

Matheo trembled and did as asked, his eyes half-lidded, as if he wasn't really seeing what was around him. Tian kept a close eye on him, but the fox was right where he wanted him to be as the hyena's fingers trailed luxuriously up his legs, tickling his inner thighs, to his crotch.

Licking his lips, Tian took a moment to enjoy the view. His cock plumped up from where it had been semi-hard already, thickening out. He had a small sheath and a moderately sized cock, but it wasn't about what he was packing that mattered. It never had mattered, not in the slightest, no.

Love and lust were about far more than that, after all.

Matheo grunted as the hyena's fingers traced a path up, brushing the fur of his crotch, where it was a little thicker and fluffier around the base of his sheath. His sheath housed a larger cock than his dominant's, though they didn't exactly compare things like that: it was just a fact. His shaft was much thicker around also when the knot was fully engorged, but it was soft at that time, no more than a subtle rise, if that, at the base of his dick.

The tip of the fox's cock was more tapered, as if to pry open a partner, and the smooth nature of the shaft practically invited Tian's paw to slide up it. The sheath tugged along with it for a moment before his paw moved too far, a prickle of sensation running through the fox.

"Mmmph…"

He grunted into his gag. Yet Matheo didn't want to spend a moment more on sound alone, panting lightly, his tongue trying to loll from his mouth. Of course, it could not, not with the gag in the way, although it didn't really register in his mind that there was something stopping him.

The fox was lost as his master pawed at his shaft, rubbing smoothly up and down the length, teasing him. It was not enough to get him off, not even with the butt plug snug and grinding against his prostate, but it was enough to get him achingly hard and wanting. Matheo whined and tried to twist his head, though it didn't offer him any relief.

He was just there to bear through it, grunting lightly. Pleasure tightened inside him with a feral rush and urge, yet there was nowhere for it to go. His tail tried to wag, to do something, anything, to appease his dominant partner, yet Matheo was not to influence what Tian did to him.

It was Tian's scene. Tian could decide. He just hoped his master wouldn't edge him and edge him for hours upon hours, although that had a certain lure to it too. Perhaps he'd have to suggest that to Tian at another time – when he wasn't tied up.

So, the fox merely groaned, ears splaying out, though the hyena ignored each and every one of his demonstrations. There was nothing Matheo could do to persuade him, without words, to do something different, for Tian already had an idea of how he wanted their scene to go.

He watched, hungrily, as his fox quivered before him. It was a thing of beauty, truly, to watch Matheo coming undone, as if he was unravelling. And yet sometimes those cords of tightness within his body and mind needed to be unravelled, the threads spinning free so relaxation could be woven back into it. He worked his paw up and down the fox's cock. Although it was a simple motion, it was how Matheo's shaft pulsed under his paw that was truly what Tian was looking for.

Throb.

Tian licked his lips, giving a little squeeze.

Throb.

The hyena pumped up the butt plug another notch, watching his partner's nostrils flare for a suck of breath.

Throb.

Matheo thrust, his buttocks pushing up, spearing his cock into Tian's paw.

They were such small things and yet they all formed an image the hyena was hungry for. He wanted it, every last sliver of detail, licking his lips. He was drooling, he knew it, and yet he still couldn't stop himself.

"I think you need to cum," Tian said, as if it was merely par for the course. "But this is going to be on my terms, pet. Lay there. You don't need to do a single thing."

He worked his paw, for the motion was a familiar one to him. There was nothing special about jacking off a partner, but he leaned into it a little, pushing over the fox's body. The hyena's elbow dropped to the bed, so he was even closer to Matheo, able to feel the shift of his body and how the bed dipped and rose with every twist of the fox.

Matheo whimpered, not really knowing what was going on. He dug his teeth into the gag, straining to stay in place, yet he could no more do that than he could prevent the passage of time.

His master had him, the fox thought dimly. As long as he was with his master, he was safe. And his master would make sure his needs were met.

Matheo just didn't always know what those needs of his were. So, Tian brought them to the forefront anyway.

"Mmm… Hmm… Nngghhh…"

Matheo strained to groan, yet any sounds the fox managed to make were dim and muffled. He drooled against the gag but barely noticed the sheen of saliva at the corners of his lips, how his tongue flicked and pulled. In such a position, with his mouth filled like that, he couldn't swallow effectively – and neither did he need to.

It just felt good, so good, just to have his rump stuffed. Matheo may well have preferred the hyena's cock to be ground up under his tail, perfectly stretching his tail hole and driving deep, but the plug was just as good. All because it came from his dominant partner, all from him.

Matheo panted more heavily, chest rising and falling in sharp, needy gulps of breath. Yet it was as if the air itself was stabbing deep into his lungs as he huffed and heaved, liquid heat pooling at his crotch.

With a strangled, broken cry, muted by the ball gag, he ejaculated, losing control and spending his seed a moment before the rush of pleasure hit him. It swelled from him in a throbbing surge and he made a mess of the hyena's paw as spurt after spurt of slick fox cum drooled down his length.

"There's a good boy," Tian praised him, admiring his fox as he creamed himself. "Such a messy pet you are. You're going to have to cum again if you want to be really good though."

Matheo didn't catch his words, although the hyena was quick enough to take charge of the next stage. He pumped the fox's cock more rapidly, almost ruthlessly, not allowing him those moments of respite to take care of himself, to rest between rounds. Historically, Matheo had always needed a little more time to recharge than Tian needed, but that had all been well and good when the hyena liked thrusting into the fox's wet maw, grinding his cock over his tongue. Spending orgasm after orgasm straight down Matheo's throat, his shaft shoved deep, so his crotch pressed all the way up to the fox's lips, the fur there tickling a little.

Yet the fox didn't get that time to rest that he needed, squirming and grunting as pleasure with a tinge of pain bit into his loins. He groaned, eyes fluttering open once more, but he didn't want to stop it. No, he wanted to be a good boy, a very good boy. Above all else, Matheo simply wanted to please his master.

In submitting, Matheo could no longer remember what had worried him so much before, what had been weighing on his mind. Had it even been all that important to begin with?

It couldn't have been, although he didn't feel quite as if he was able to bear through his master rubbing his shaft. But just when he thought the hyena was going to, at the very least, allow him a few moments, things ramped up.

"It's been a while since we've played with one of these, pet," Tian said, plugging in a vibrating massage wand with the big, smooth, rounded end. "You loved this before. But how long will you hold out before you make a mess again?"

His paw was still dirty from the fox's cream and Tian grinned widely, crudely rubbing it off on the fox's muzzle. He didn't need to leave his paws all messy like that, after all, not when he had a willing pet down there to use as a rag and even less than that.

The fox quivered, muzzle twitching as he fought his urges. Yet it was not for him to deny himself as Tian carefully cupped the side of the fox's shaft that faced his belly, all so he could trap it between his paw and the massage wand. Switching it on to a low setting, he let the vibrations travel powerfully into the fox's dick, the reverberations flowing far deeper than a mere surface level.

Matheo groaned, squirming and twitching. If he'd been free to do so in the moment, he would have been thrashing, but that simply wasn't the fox's concern. He couldn't think straight in the moment and rocked his hips up, glutes tensing, his body too sensitive for the massage wand, losing control.

He grunted, tonguing the ball gag, but he didn't want to get away. Although the ball was still in his paw, he squeezed the fingers of his other paw more tightly, not wanting to stop.

He wanted to be good. And he could be good by holding out for his master, letting his body give the hyena every drop of cum Tian wanted to drain from him.

Again.

And again.

He grunted and he groaned and he struggled, yet his body could not escape the press of the massage wand, no matter how he sought relief. The fox's throat constricted and, for a few heart-stopping moments, even his chest was too tight to breathe. Yet it all came the moment he allowed himself to relax into it, to accept he didn't have any chance at changing the dominance play in that moment. He was never meant to be on top, not like that, anyway.

"My good boy," Tian praised. "What a good pet you are… Breathe… You can cum again…"

As if he'd been called to do so, a rush of pained pleasure bit through the fox's crotch and he arched helplessly, not sure what to do. His body rocked and twisted, trying to do as his master willed, spending ropes of juddering, sputtering seed over his lower abdomen. It was not as strong an orgasm in productivity as his first and Tian kept his paw out of the way that time, so not a drop of cum marked it.

He just kept going. The fox quivered and groaned and twisted with his eyes shining with moisture and, even so, the hyena kept right on going. The muscle in his arms bunched as he stood again, the fox close enough to the side of the bed for him to reach, though he rolled the dial on the massage wand, increasing the intensity bit by bit.

Tian laughed softly, delighting in his pet's antics. His thighs tensed, as if that would get him out of it, the toes on his hind paws splayed out as if they were reaching for something, tipped with short claws that were filed smooth. Yet the fox wasn't going anywhere as his cock fell semi-hard. As much as it strained to soften, Tian still forced it on, forced Matheo's body to thrum with pump after pump of what may have been, by that point, rather unwelcome pleasure.

Matheo groaned and whimpered, but Tian only knew he was making those sounds by the twitch of his muzzle and the pull of his throat, betraying him. The fox would be quiet, yet he didn't drop or squeeze the ball, so all was well.

He pressed on, grinding the massage wand up and down Matheo's shaft, even teasing it into the soft pouch of his nuts. His balls allowed him to indent them lightly, yet it was trickier to keep the massage wand in place there as Matheo fought even more vehemently. The hyena wasn't about to let him get away with that, however, and he pressed down firmly with the flat of his paw against the hyena's thigh.

"Still, pet. Still."

Matheo grunted, but he could do no more than that. He was too far gone, lost in a moment entirely of his master's design.

He needed to cum – and yet he couldn't at the same time. His mind rocked back and forth, torn between opposing feelings, yet he wasn't able to choose between them. It was not his place, not as muscles he'd never even thought about tightened. A pull ground down deep within his core and he swallowed a howl that he knew wouldn't even come out anyway, so what was the point in wasting energy on a cry like that?

The fox just needed to keep on, to hold on, to let the throbs and pulses roll through him. The strain was the worst part of it and the most exhilarating at the same time. It was hard to consider anything else as Matheo growled, his throat tight with emotion and his mouth far too wet with saliva.

"Cum for me, pet," his master encouraged, even though it was hard to hear his voice over the buzzing vibrator. "You can do it. Be a good boy for me now."

It was strange to think of such soft, gentle words coming up against rougher play. The burning ache through his body demanded relief and yet it wasn't up to the fox to thrust, to grind, to let it all leave his body. The butt plug ground up inside him, still there and feeling as if it was bigger than ever, even though he hadn't felt it getting any larger. Maybe the hyena had pumped it up when he hadn't been paying attention?

There was no way to tell and Matheo wasn't in any position to say. His maw would have been gaping if not for the gag and he closed his eyes against the strain. He had to hold on, had to push through it. Even though he thought he could hear his master saying something, he couldn't catch the words as the buzzing rang through his head, as if there was nothing else there other than the vibrations, the massage wand that brought such a coarse pleasure to his body.

Tian guided him through it, but he was not even fully confident the fox was aware of what was happening. Stripping Matheo down to nothing at all, he coaxed a final, juddering orgasm from the vulpine. Cum dribbled from his cock, all Matheo had left to give, but his cock was not even hard. It could not have been said to be a fulfilling orgasm – yet that was never what it was supposed to be.

For the aftermath was sweeter than the roughness as Tian let down his partner, keeping contact with him and grounding him while he removed the plug and the bondage, the massage wand still plugged in but set well aside.

"What a good boy…" He murmured, drawing his partner in close even though Tian's cock was still hard and wanton, shiny at the head with pre-cum. "You've done so well. Relax now."

Finally, the fox could truly relax, warmth spreading through his muscles. A delicious ache remained, from where he had fought his bondage and tried to thrust in the peak of pleasure, yet it was a good ache.

Tiredness seeped through and Matheo's eyelids closed. Tian smiled gently, cupping the fox's cheek with his paw and teasing the base of his ears. Scratching lightly, he helped his partner relax. For he'd done everything he needed to meet the fox's needs, while his own could wait a little longer, until Matheo was in a better frame of mind.

Nothing was there to stop them, bringing light and dark together in the perfect twist of BDSM and, perhaps, rather unconventional relationships.

"Rest now."

Matheo breathed, a smile fluttering over his lips, finally free of the gag.

He'd pay Tian back in blowjob after blowjob, even though he didn't really need to. For what they had in their relationship, power play or otherwise, transcended the realm of mere sex and favours.

Together, they knew one another. Together, they could do anything.

Together, they'd overcome everything.

With a big dose of pleasure at play too, of course.

Cock Worship

"I didn't think you were going to be quite this big…"

Hayes grunted, the sergal down on his knees before the big stud. Of course, he'd known a stallion like Ametrine was going to be large, but he hadn't considered just how big he was.

The chestnut horse's cock swung down, faintly, in a gentle arc under its own weight. And what a beast of a cock it was… The sergal licked his lips, his long, slender tongue lashing out and back into his wedge-shaped muzzle, yet the moment was not about him. Hayes would have had all eyes on him otherwise, with his thickly furred body and long, fluffy tail with the springy fluff right at the tip. His aquamarine blue fur and the creamy off-white of his chest and belly often caught the eye for their striking lines, the upper side of his muzzle blue while his lower jaw traced that same line of white.

Ametrine rumbled a chuckle, the stallion comfortably sitting back on the sofa, which looked rather small now that the big horse was there. Churring lightly under his breath, Hayes rubbed his cheek against the horse's thigh, his own cock throbbing and trying to gain some manner of attention. The sergal, however, simply didn't want to waste a moment on his own lust when Ametrine was there to please.

"And how big did you think I was before you gave me four beers and dragged me back to your place?" The stallion said, his tone warm with good humour. "Not that those beers touched me, mind you."

"I… Uh…"

Hayes blushed and shook his head, suddenly feeling ever so slightly foolish. Just what had he thought?

He'd just wanted the stud and wanted to see what he could do to get him back to his apartment.

Hayes hadn't honestly thought it would work, not coming back from the bar with laughter on their lips and hope in the crisp, cool night air. They were down in a tourist town near the beach, though he could tell from Ametrine's accent that he was a local. He just wasn't sure how he hadn't seen the horse around before, but it was not unusual for some guys to keep to themselves.

He turned his attention back to Ametrine's cock. The horse had shoved his jeans down, at the sergal's bidding, to show off his hard, throbbing length. Still, it did not seem to have grown to its full size, the flat tip so big that the sergal was not at all sure how he was going to take it into his mouth beyond a few inches, even if he really wanted to. Oh, how he longed to feel it bearing over his tongue, grinding into the back of his throat... Yet sometimes the realities of physical limitations made it difficult to make things happen.

The length of horse cock was mostly pink and fleshy, though there were some grey patches on it too, with some speckles of grey close to the base, past the medial ring. The throbbing pull of the medial ring twitched around his cock and the sergal reverently brushed it with his fingers, curling his fingers around as much of the girth as he could. He may as well have not done so at all for it was laughable just how small his paws were in comparison to the stallion's.

"Why don't you take a taste?" Ametrine invited him, the red stallion shooting him a charming grin, completely in his element. "Come on, darling, you know you want to. You don't have to do anything you don't wanna do, but you're the one that pulled me back here. I think it's more than fair to say. I don't mind riding you too, if you'd rather see about ploughing my ass."

The sergal quivered. Oh, that was almost a hotter thought than taking the stallion under his tail, but he didn't know what he wanted more. It was hard to decide when faced with too many pleasurable choices, all at once.

"Mmm, ah..." Hayes floundered for words, rubbing the back of his neck. "I think... Heh, you've really caught me off-guard here. I don't know what to say!"

Yet Ametrine didn't need to be passive there, not as he stood and gently drew the sergal along with him. Ametrine's jeans were not shoved down further than his cock, not even letting the stallion's heavy nuts out yet, so he was still able to shuffle. He tipped Hayes' head up a little so he could kiss him, invading the sergal's mouth with a broad, fleshy tongue.

The sergal moaned and quivered against him, his body so much smaller and lither than the stallion's muscled bulk. Ametrine's abdomen was riddled with muscle, though there was so much width to him, easily dwarfing the sergal.

Yet it was better right then and there in the moment, kissing him deeply, letting his slenderer tongue twitch and pull and wind around the stallion's, merely caught up in the moment of exploration. There was nothing either of them "had" to do and having that expectation lifted from his shoulders at the very least reassured the sergal. As much as he wanted to take the stallion's cock up his ass, there was only so much he could do without a great deal more preparation.

"Mm... Okay," Hayes breathed, breaking the kiss briefly, head spinning. "Let's... The bedroom's down the hall."

They staggered there, wound up in one another's arms. The sergal's tail alternately helped balance him and wrapped around the stallion's waist, curling around just to show off how far it could bend, how much it could twist. Even then, he longed to have

Ametrine pressed up against him as much as possible, to not allow even an inch of spare space between him and the stallion's body remain for too long.

When they tumbled on to Hayes' bed together, however, everything heated up just as the sergal had wanted. His heart surged and lust rose, his cock pushing from his sheath. It sprung out wantonly into his shorts, but he didn't have the chance to grope at it, not as the horse took control.

It was so very much easier to let the stallion take the lead, even though the sergal knew well enough what he was doing too. He wasn't exactly inexperienced at sex. Yet there was something about knowing he was getting something other than what he'd expected that ticked all the right boxes for him.

He didn't have to take something, after all, that he wasn't ready for. And that was okay too, as he groaned, Ametrine working off his shorts and dragging his shirt over his head. The sergal tried to squirm and help him along with it, although there wasn't much he could do besides show his eagerness and readiness as clearly as he was able.

"Come here," Ametrine nickered, standing to draw off his own shirt and also let his jeans slide down, working them off along with his underwear. "You don't have to do much… But a little taste can't hurt, can it?"

The stallion smirked playfully as his cock bounced up, throbbing with a ring of desire. The head had flared out a little more, though Ametrine didn't draw attention to it, not as the sergal, as if hypnotised, folded to his knees before the stud.

"Mm, that I can definitely do," Hayes murmured huskily. "Let me see you…"

The stallion's cock was so much bigger than his, pulsing lightly as the sergal cradled it in his paws. He stroked them down to the base, marvelling at the sheer weight of a cock like that, yet he longed to adore it.

So, his lips slid around the head, suckling lightly and pulling, though Hayes had to open his jaws a lot wider than he would have normally just to squeeze it inside. It was a lot fleshier and spongier than any cock tip he'd ever had the luxury of taking before, though he was not bothered in the slightest by it. It was just something more to play with, sweeping his tongue around the head to tease the glands, playing and exploring.

His cock, however, had been freed when the stallion had helped him out of his clothes. In the open air, it throbbed and bounced faintly, yet there was no comparison to the might of Ametrine's shaft. It was never meant to stand in comparison to him, for they were quite different creatures.

Still, Hayes sank into the moment, letting nothing else exist for him other than Ametrine's length, adoring the meat and sliding his mouth down as far as he could along the beastly girth. It throbbed over his tongue, forcing it down within his mouth, and he could barely swallow, eyes watering as Hayes practically drove it into the back of his throat.

"Mmph…"

He let out a needy groan, although he needed more, so very much more. The rush of heat in that massive member was beyond anything he could have imagined, even though the sergal had been with stallions before. Just how was Ametrine so much bigger? It had his head swimming pleasantly, as if he was drifting into another realm, somewhere that things could be smoother, flowing more easily. A trickle of pre-cum dropped on to his tongue and he worked his tongue, striving his best to swallow it down. With the thick length of meat stuffed into his muzzle, it was more difficult than it had to be.

"That's it… Mmm, wow, that feels good," Ametrine groaned, his tail swishing in a slow drag of hair against the backs of his thighs. "Get your tongue up against the underside, ah… Yes. Just like that."

The stallion nickered eagerly, as much an active participant in every moment, though the slow roll of his hips speared his cock ever so slightly into the sergal's throat. Hayes gulped around the flared head, ignoring how his eyes watered.

He wished it could go deeper, though he had to settle for sweeping his paws up and down the fat length, fingers curling around, folding and rubbing. Hayes committed every inch of the stallion's shaft to memory, even letting his fingers dance over the soft fold of the stud's sheath. It was looser around the base of his cock, as if there was even more of the beast to be shown, though Hayes didn't think he could handle much more.

He just wanted to stay down there forever, sucking and slurping, his jaw aching even as he grew increasingly familiar with the shape of the shaft. Pulling back all the way to the head, Hayes took a little more time, his eyes falling half-lidded, not seeing anything before him but the monster cock.

He didn't let the head pop free of his lips, however, as he slurped around it, messily drooling and moaning as he rubbed up and down the length firmly. His palms bounced over the rather girthy medial ring, which was a lot thicker than anything he'd seen on any other anthro, of any other species. Ametrine nickered and stomped above him, although the sergal didn't feel out of place or unsafe at all.

Despite the horse being so much larger and bulkier than him, he was content there, wrapped in arousal. But only when his fingers folded around his own member did the stallion gently bid him to rise, drawing him on to the bed.

"How do you want me?" Ametrine groaned, the stallion clearly more than a little pent-up and ready. "Riding you?"

The sergal flashed him a grin, heart hammering.

"Mmm, yes, that sounds *amazing*."

The word left him with a sense of relish and, in a moment, he was on his back on his bed with the stallion straddling his hips. He'd never had such a big, muscular anthro on top of him like that and a surge of something lustful but electric powered through him. Hayes licked his lips, his long tail slinking up over the stallion's leg and tightening there, curling around as many times as it felt able and flexible enough to.

He positioned his cock so Ametrine could sink on to it, though the sergal only regretted he didn't quite get a good view of the stallion's thick doughnut of flesh spreading around his shaft. His cock slid deep and the sergal gasped, though he would not have said it took his breath away. On the contrary, he gasped and ragged in needy gulp of breath after breath, straining for all he felt was his to take.

His chest heaved and he grasped the stallion's cock as Ametrine rode him, that slick, tight heat wrapped around his dick. Yet the stallion's member was still something he could worship, taking it in both paws and by far not being a passive player in their mutual pleasure.

He might not have easily been able to take the stallion's cock, but he could squeeze it and rub it, even kneading his fingers into the softer sponge of the head. It flared out increasingly, showing off the stallion's promiscuity and virility in one fell swoop, and Hayes moaned, longing for that cum shot.

"I can't wait until you blow your load," Hayes murmured huskily. "Yes… More… Come on, stud, ride me!"

Ametrine was more than ready to do as he willed, wanting them both to enjoy their lust. The stallion's tail swished, dragging over the sergal's legs, though the moment was for both and he rocked his hips. Sinking to his knees rather than a crouch, he kept Hayes' cock as deep as possible, grinding down on to him as if the two of them had been fucking for years already.

Yet it was their first time together and Hayes savoured every moment, wishing, in a way, it would go on forever. He didn't want to miss a thing and yet it would take many more sexual liaisons with Ametrine to truly understand the depth of his attraction to the stallion and what pulled him into the stud's arms, time after time again. It wasn't the stallion's dick or even his body, despite that being the first thing that the sergal had seen of him in the bar.

His body, not his cock. Though the latter could have been exciting too…

No. It was the stallion's personality. That cheeky glint shining in his eye as he rode Hayes' cock. The softness with which he held the sergal when their fun was over. Even the snap of excitement that came with the stallion's spontaneity.

There was much more for Hayes to learn and know about the horse, but one night could not cover everything. It was just to be enjoyed.

The stud's breath caught in his throat as his chest juddered visibly, yet they were both close at the same time, so very close. The need to cum rolled through the sergal and, if he had not been as caught up as he was in jacking off his massive member, he would have cum at once inside Ametrine's ass. The stallion's tight hole squeezed and even seemed to ripple along him, as if he was controlling even the muscles inside his ass, pulling up the sergal's length. Of course, that was not so – yet the moment was such that reality and fantasy blurred in a delicious cocktail of lust.

"Ugh…" Hayes gasped, squirming under Ametrine, holding back even as the monster cock throbbed in his hands. "So close… How about you? Let me… Mm, wanna see you cum."

The stallion was Hayes' only focus, yet he had nothing to worry about. Not as Ametrine rocked his hips, clearly torn between shoving his hips down and thrusting into the sergal's grasp. It was decidedly a wonderful conundrum to find himself in, though all for their mutual benefit.

Ametrine's cock throbbed and the sergal got a front-row seat to the cumulation of his lust, that beast of a member jerking within both of his paws. Thick, creamy ropes of seed shot from the head, spurt after spurt, splattering Hayes' chest. He didn't mind the slick mess, finding the stream of seed soaking into his fur an added sensation to a cacophony of lust, his own desire rising inside him like a flash flood.

His orgasm may not have been as demanding as the stallion's, as further ropes of seed painted Hayes' chest, but it was his pleasure to soak in every last little moment, even the stickiness of cum drooling into his fur. Ecstasy flared, like the head of Ametrine's cock, and the sergal let out a breathless moan, as if his lust would not quite leap from his lips.

It was okay if he was quiet, however, panting heavily, his chest rising and falling in a rhythm he, at least, could follow. Hayes' eyelids fluttered, lost in the moment, though he was dimly aware of Ametrine's fingers curling around his shoulder, holding him in place. Yet it was reassuring too, a comforting weight, and he exhaled more gently, spending his seed straight up into the stallion's rump.

Ametrine's tail lashed over his thighs as they both sank into it, letting everything roll through. They could take the moment exactly as they pleased, but there would be many more moments like that too.

The sergal hummed pleasantly under his breath, massaging the length of the stallion's member. He squeezed his fingers around, testing the stud's sensitivity, though he didn't want to push Ametrine too far. The stallion grunted throatily, leaning over the sergal and demonstrating surprising flexibility as he trapped his cock, bouncing lightly, between their bodies.

The heat of him sank into Hayes and, in that moment, the sergal wanted it to be so much more than cock worship. It was not all about him lusting for the stallion for his body or what he was packing, but so much more than that. Even if that was not what they had started the night looking for, it was how it ended.

And that was okay too, the slick mess of the stallion's seed smeared into their fur and between their bodies, though the stallion was ready to go again already. The stallion nickered softly and kissed Hayes, stealing his breath away.

In worship, they found something more.

And the two of them were set to explore many experiences together, beyond their wildest dreams.

Barn Bang

Eokia exhaled, the pegasus' wings spreading out against the back of the barn, his long, golden tail swishing back and forth against the rear side of his legs. He'd had his eye on Fletcher for quite some time, although he hadn't known how to "start things" with the gorgeous sheep. The stallion had coaxed out of the sheep that he had Dorper Hair (a specific type of sheep) lineage, which came through in his black face and the shorter, thicker curl of his wool.

That was cute, so cute, and the ram had long, dark eyelashes too. They were almost feminine, yet the set of the sheep's body was ever so slightly stocky as he leaned in against the horse's body.

"So," Eokia breathed, sweeping his hands down the ram's back and resting them in the small of his back. "Is that a yes to the date then? I hope so…"

Fletcher let out a soft bleat, quivering against the pegasus. It didn't feel real, not being pressed up against him like that with a light drizzle in the air, some of the moisture beading on his wool. It should have been embarrassing to let out the high-pitched bleat, yet it felt okay, as it was Eokia there with him.

Did the stallion know how much he'd been watching him since he'd started work at the farm? It was good work and easy work, the kind of work where he didn't have to think too much about what he was doing, except when he was operating machinery. It all came easily to him and Fletcher enjoyed being out in the fresh air too.

That day, however, Eokia had asked him out for a drink – or a coffee, the stallion had said, for he had not known whether the sheep drank or not – and Fletcher's heart had kicked into overdrive. When Eokia had nickered and drawn him in against his taller body, broader across the chest with muscle but still with narrower, finer hips, he hadn't known what to say.

Yet the stallion did not trap him, his arms held loosely around the ram so Fletcher could have escaped if he'd wanted to. There was always a chance for him to leave and he appreciated not being penned in, though he likely wouldn't have been as interested in the beautiful pegasus stallion as he was if he'd had any thought in his mind that the stallion would have tried to force him.

"Yeah…" He finally said, though the ram still didn't know how or why the stallion would have been interested in him. "You're… Yeah, I'd love to go for a drink with you."

Eokia grinned, his wings fluttering a little, a golden feather drifting off. His coat of short hair was an off-white, though he worked hard to keep it in good condition. He was sure Fletcher struggled too with the white of his wool, for there was little either of them could do to hide any marks or dirt that hopped a ride on their bodies.

"That's great," he said warmly, chest vibrating lightly as he groaned. "So, what do you say about going to that little pub down in the village? You know, Watson's? It's supposed to have some really nice local ciders."

Fletcher's attention perked up, but blood roared in his ears. A smile pulled at his lips, stretching them wider and wider.

For he wasn't quiet listening to what the stallion was saying. It was hard to, especially with that surge of lust in his body, how it pulled somewhere deep down in his loins. He grunted and licked his lips, yet the stallion was a good foot and a half taller than him, so it was not as easy as all that just to reach up and kiss him.

The ram was not all that bold, not usually. Yet it felt right in that moment, especially as something pushed out lower down on his body, against his belly.

It was not something of the sheep's, however, and Eokia blushed and tried to pull away, the stallion, comically, struggling to squirm suddenly from the sheep.

"I don't think we're going to make it all the way down there," the ram breathed, eyes twinkling with friendly glee. "I didn't think you'd be *that* interested in me, pony..."

Eokia squirmed and nickered throatily, though his voice was higher pitched than normal.

"I... Uh..." He fought for words, chortling on a laugh and rubbing the back of his neck even as Fletcher rested his hands on the horse's hips. "Well, you know, I thought I could be all cool and suave and pull you against me... Hah, well, you are really cute, you know!"

For Eokia's shaft was swelling, plumping out his sheath and making an obvious, if subtle, bulge in his jeans. If they had not been a little looser around the crotch, it may not have been something the sheep could have felt, his clothes keeping his length under control. The stallion's cock, understandably, was massive, although it wasn't something he usually made a big deal about.

There was little he could do to hide it, even if he wanted to be discreet about it and not scare the ram off. Yet it was Eokia who ended up on the back hoof, blushing as the sheep stretched up on the tips of his own cloven hooves to kiss the underside of his chin.

"Well, let's see where this goes then," Fletcher breathed. "You good?"

He checked in with the pegasus, whose wings shuffled and ruffled against his back, trying to fold in. Yet he didn't want to shift away, wanting to see where the sheep wanted to take things.

For maybe it was not all about Eokia making the first move but both of them coming together in the soft grey of the countryside, exactly the way they were supposed to.

Fletcher barely even knew what he was doing, his legs trembling a little despite his desire. He didn't want to give up now that he had found his boldness, lips parted slightly as he palmed the stallion's bulge. His fingers cupped the rising swell and he dragged the digits up, teasing Eokia's rising throb while he fiddled with his button and zip.

It took the sheep a few moments to slide them down and the stallion let out a throaty nicker as his erection was freed. Both of them helped, though Fletcher giggled lightly at how eager they both were.

"Uh, I've never done anything like this before, heh," he blurted out, too forward and still wanting to let that side of himself free. "But I wanna… If that's not too much."

Eokia snorted, pulling the sheep with him, though his lips curved into a smile even as he backed into the barn through the back door.

"Ah… Yeah, yeah, I want to," he said. "But I want to go out with you too, you know. Not just sex. Just want to make that really clear."

The ram smiled and nodded, but the moment was for them as he yanked down his own work trousers, which were a little tougher and rougher than the stallion's clothing. He wanted to protect his wool, but it was clear just how much smaller his cock was in comparison to the stallion's, even though it was big for his size at seven-and-a-half or eight-ish inches.

The stallion's cock, on the other hand, was big and fat with a meaty medial ring. It was mostly pink with a speckling of grey around the head, as if it tempted at mottling without actually going all the way. The sheep groaned, lips parting, and sat over the horse's legs as Eokia sat back on a bale of straw.

Outside, the rain pattered down against the roof of the barn, but they were secluded there away from prying eyes as the ram rolled his hips, grinding lightly against Eokia's shaft. He enjoyed the feeling and moaned lightly, rubbing their cocks together, using his hands too so nothing went to waste.

For Fletcher, after all, it was all about the moment, letting it wash over him. It was unconventional and, later, he'd wonder just how he'd been able to be so bold at the time – yet it didn't matter. He could press on, the stallion's lips moulding softly to his, though it was Eokia who made the moment so much more.

They kissed as Eokia led, letting the sheep do as much as he wanted. All they were doing, however, was just a teaser for what they were going to do together after their date, tempting and teasing at a little more. For there would always be a little more, other ways to push limits and take a chance or two.

They just needed to be on the same page to take it all well enough in hand, grunting and groaning. They could be just as they were, two barnyard animals satisfying their lust in the heat of the moment, enjoying every throb and tingle of desire.

Coffee would be nice and so would a drink together. Just like the movie night and the bowling and the walks out in the countryside. They'd head down to the city too, just to see what was out there that could catch their interest, but it would always be the two of them.

Frotting, right then and there, was all that mattered for their first time and their first leap together. Eokia sensually rolled his hips and ground against the sheep, enjoying every thrust, though more so the press of Fletcher's lips against his. The sheep kissed him desperately, their tongues flicking and curling up against one another, though the exchange of saliva only deepened the moment.

For it was that afternoon, just as they were wrapping up work for the day, that the first spark of connection between them flared to life. From there, it would grow and grow, their throbbing lengths grinding against one another, luxuriating where they were. Fletcher gasped into the horse's mouth, ears twitching to take in the rustle of feathers, yet he did not dare break the moment as the pegasus' wings shifted anxiously.

They were both close, the lust of sneaking around and thrusting themselves into the unknown getting to them both. The sheep's cock drooled a dribble of pre-cum and he panted heavily, breaking the kiss and tucking his muzzle into the crook of the stallion's neck.

It felt safe there, where he could rest and exult in the moment. Every flicker of passion swept through him, building to a crescendo, though it was all Fletcher could do to contain himself.

He didn't want to lose control, not that quickly, though the horse pulled him back suddenly, his back arching as he pushed his hips forward, even from his seated position. Eokia grunted and grabbed his cock suddenly, almost breaking their contact, but the pegasus was not quick enough to stop his orgasm from jetting off. For a stallion's climax was erratic, pulsating crudely, thick rolls of cum travelling up the full length of his cock as he spent himself everywhere.

The ram barely even realised the mess that was being made, not even as ropes of stallion seed splattered up against his chest and marked their bellies. It even soaked into their trousers, the stallion's jeans holding up ever so slightly better – but not by much.

It was a mess to deal with, although there was only so much they could do, panting heavily in the aftermath, laughing lightly. They'd deal with it all, but that did not make the mess a bad thing, even if they'd have to fob off questions about their state and say they'd got soaked with a broken hosepipe. Nobody really bought it, but no one worked out what they had really been doing either.

So, that was enough for Eokia and Fletcher, the start of their relationship together. Time would roll on and they'd always remember that first time, even if their future was set to be even wilder.

Together, they had the whole world to explore.

Transforming Convention

Gage swallowed hard, though going out onto the dance floor at his first furry convention with a few drinks in him already should not have, really, been the strangest thing in the world. Alas, it was a gathering of people from all walks of life, yes, but quite often primarily those that spent a lot of time behind a computer screen, a little set aside from the "normality" of the world. Gage was one of those people, shifting his weight from foot to foot, his old trainers, as comfortable as they were, seeming out of place where everyone was in some kind of furry paraphernalia.

Tails were everywhere, the anthropomorphic fandom in full swing, celebrating the coming together of like-minded people, though all skin colours, races, cultures, genders and more were there. There were no lines to be drawn between them, all coming there for the same thing, to get away from the grind of the real world, normal life, though such holidays and breaks should not have been to escape anything. Yet escapism was so present in life, whether one wanted to get far away from their day-to-day lives or had found some way to make it work for them.

Gage hoped he could get there one day, yet it was still awkward there, eyes wandering, lights flashing, the music pumping. The bass throbbed through him and he laughed softly to himself, thinking that there would be complaints from other hotel guests if they kept going like that, though he didn't know what else they expected from a furry con. Even he'd known it would be loud and proud, celebrating all that the fandom was for the few days that they could come together, bringing furries together from all around the world.

"Hey – you having a good time?"

Dale didn't wait for him to say anything, even if he was hard to recognise in fursuit – even a partial.

Wearing a feline head with quivering whiskers in a silver tabby base, the stripes were laboriously highlighted, just at the edges, with purple and blue, giving him a unique twist on a common animal. The paws of his suit smoothed over Gage's wrists as he was grabbed, dragged into the midst of the dance floor, Dale whooping, glow sticks around his neck and wrists, riding high on the thrill of the con.

For that was what it was all about and, where possible, it was about giving oneself over to the fun of it all, wherever that could be done. For there was always a caveat, different people enjoying different things at their own pace, though there was never much point at all in being one of those people sitting in the lobby playing a popular MMORPG on their laptops, as keen as Gage was on that game too in his free time. But he was there to see people and he laughed aloud, louder that time, as Dale spun him, wearing feetpaws too, tail bobbing back and forth, catching Gage's eye.

Dale didn't know how much Gage was into him, but Gage hoped, maybe, that he'd find the courage at the con, dancing together, laughing at how uncoordinated they were, flailing more than actually dancing. They didn't have to be perfect there, however, and there were few out on the dance floor who could have been said to be good dancers by any conventional standards, though those in fursuit were out and proud about it more than others. They twisted and cavorted, whether in full suit or partials, amazing Gage so much with their lithe antics that sometimes Dale had to turn his attention back to what they were doing, where they were.

The music dropped, a deep, pumping bass throbbing through Gage, lips parted, eyes feeling like they caught Dale's, even through the mask. The feline head stared back at him, but he felt the warmth of the other furry through the hand on his forearm, tightening all of a sudden.

"Dale?"

"Gage, I…

They pressed in, moving as one, but what was to transpire there would not need to ever be considered something to be explained the next day. Gage giggled as his lips brushed those of the suit, but that was not what he'd planned, not what he'd wanted, heart pounding, dizzy all of a sudden, though he had not had anywhere near his limit in alcohol, always careful. Dale fumbled against him, a handpaw dropping to his waist, his hips, feeling warmer there than it had before.

Wait… Was he supposed to feel warm through the suit? Gage's brow furrowed, others around them shifting, the heaving mass of the dance floor suddenly becoming even more restrictive. He didn't understand what was happening, steadying Dale as he dropped off balance, yet he swore the lips of the suit were moving, panting, mewling.

"Dale? Dale, are you okay?"

Whereas things were very okay for everyone there, they were different, very different, Gage's eyes dropping to the handpaws, how they curled around his wrists, clinging to him as if for dear life. There was something wrong there, something different – not wrong but changing, the claws feeling sharper, smaller, more pinprick-like, like those of an actual anthropomorphic cat…

No…

But yes. Something had shifted in the fabric of time and being, at the convention, and there was no going back as tabby fur, all stripes touched with blue and purple, spread all over Dale's body. He howled, tail lashing the air, suddenly possessing the muscles to use it, though Gage quickly rushed in, closing what little distance remained between them as Dale threatened to drop to his knees.

"Dale! Dale, what's happening? Are you okay?"

The beat of the music rose and rose, throbbing through the room, though there was no holding back from it, no evading it, not as Dale tried to stagger up again, his feetpaws now actual hind paws, pushing up onto his toes, his body adjusting itself into a digitigrade form. He panted heavily, a raspy, pink tongue lolling out, though Gage could not resist a soft cry of wonder.

Little did he know what was to happen to him too, his fursuit lanyard bumping against something softer as he glanced down, finally, at his own chest. Yet he hardly knew where to place his attention as those around, some grinding, others merely dancing, cried out and panted, changes coming upon them too. Even as the prickling of pink fur, in the pattern of an Alsatian dog with a white underbelly and softer hued markings, sprung to life all over him, his fingernails pressing together into dark claws, his hands somewhere between the paws that he was familiar with and paw-like hands, which were more typical in the furry fandom.

He would have stumbled back, jaw open in shock, if not for Dale holding onto him tightly, keeping him there, the feline anthro's green eyes fixed on him. He couldn't drag his attention away, whimpering softly as his body gurgled and churned. There was no pain to speak of, not as a tail sprouted from the base of his spine, pushing down the back of his trousers, his face bulging, distorting his vision for the moment. Of course, he had not had a fursuit head on for the "magic" to take hold of, not like with Dale.

Others faced the same, other dogs, cats, horses, various birds, even some dinosaurs – and more – transforming into every furry species that could ever have been imagined. All were anthropomorphic, yet muzzles already were locking together in lustful passion, tongues tangling, grinding in against one another. They had to get out their lust in some way before it was too late to do so and Gage whimpered, a pink tongue lolling out over the edge of his lips.

Was he…his fursona? A rush of heat flared up in his cheeks, ears pulling up to the top of his head, transformation progressing quickly as Dale, who was so loud and bold in real life, clung to him. Yet Gage's body fleshed out with muscle, despite his pink body, breaking conventions and traditions as he showed off just what a canine with his kind of blocky, yet refined, muzzle could do, a natural grin pulling at his lips.

Something burned through him that wasn't embarrassment, but he needed no further explanation of what was happening as Dale pushed up against him. In that moment, it was as if they were the only two in the room, breath catching in their throats, eyes finally locking as their fursonas.

Time slowed.

They could have stopped, held back, not leaned into what everyone around them was already in various stages of, yet it was not to be. Or it was to be – in the best of ways.

Their lips met, moaning into the kiss, paws roaming, though they still retained the dexterity of fingers like human hands, even if they were somewhere in the middle: anthropomorphic. It was a beautiful concept, combining love and self-expression with human nature and influence, bringing their passions together as Gage's heart pounding.

What was he doing? There, with Dale? But it felt right, so very right, throwing caution to the wind, holding tightly onto the cat anthro as if he thought that he might lose him in the chaos of the dance floor. The music had softened, only slightly, to a pulsing driving beat that undercut the current of lust and sexuality in the air, those around them throwing themselves full force into the passion that their new, anthro bodies finally allowed.

Tails and legs tangled, yowls filling the air – but all Gage had eyes for was Dale, pulling his T-shirt off over his head, exposing his bare chest, the creamy-white of his fur where the stripes ended. The hardness in Dale's jeans, no longer suited to dancing, made him bold, becoming more like his canine-sona by the second, finding that dog-like courage, even if he was still Gage, very much so.

It wasn't everyone else "doing it" that made Gage bold as he freed the swelling length of Dale's hard-on, but something inside him that had changed. The feline clung to him with a meow and a yowl, hanging off his shoulders, as the dog-anthro chuckled throatily, stroking his shaft slowly, bringing him to full hardness. Neither of them were virgins, but every sensation in their new bodies was fresh and stark in that world, making them want it all the more, whimpering, grunting, moaning, pushing in closer together as if they were the only two in the world that mattered.

To them, that was all that mattered, Dale's throbbing length pushing into Gage's handpaw, though it was different, not quite as smooth as expected, almost as if his anthro body had given him the semblance of feline "spines" or "barbs" too. Yet on an anthro body, that was never how Dale had designed them or imagined himself to be, so they were left gentle, best to please a partner rather than being too accurate to species.

Gage, however… He blushed, smirking a little, still himself but also his 'sona, his shaft hardening, a sheath like Dale's tugging around the base of his shaft as it pulled back from his growing length. It was tapered at the tip, showing his true features as an anthro, but it was the bulge that would show at the base, when all came through, that he was keenest to explore.

How would that feel? Would he do it right there? It felt right, squeezing Dale's shaft lightly, experimenting with what felt best. Some couples (or more) around them pressed up to the wall, some half over the stage, the DJ even moaning as someone sucked the dragon's shaft under the booth (it was obvious by how the wolf furry had left their tail sticking out, wagging all the while), the event going on as if it was the most normal thing in the world. Yet maybe it was the transformations themselves that had teased down the lowering of inhibitions, bringing tongues tangling together, rampant shafts out and on show, hard lengths wanting something more.

If they'd been clearer and more coherent in their minds, however, they would have realised that there were only males in there, whether they were there by design or by pure accident. They came together, lust throbbing, passion rising, hot, heaving bodies filling the space, spreading to gain their own room even over the chairs that had been stacked on one side of the stage.

"G-Gage?"

The feline was not less confident as a furry than he was as a man, just a man, but he blushed more, Gage taking command, a strong canine anthro, pushing on. His tongue wrapped around the cat's as they came together, their shafts out, proudly demonstrating their lust, though any sense of shyness that they felt only heightened their experience. More so then than any other time, it was where they were meant to be, what they were meant to be, panting, grunting, softly pushing up together with a strong handpaw to guide them together.

Somehow, they ended up down on the floor, laughing together as Gage twisted out of his jeans in a mess, trying to strip down, so much shredded clothing already littering the dance hall. The music thrummed through, providing an uncurrent to shared lust, bodies humping, grinding, fur all on show. The lights kept it dim, flashing swathes cutting across bodies in the midst of passion, blue and green and purple and so many other colours casting a brief glow over what had come to pass down there. But they did not need full light to see what was going on as Gage growled softly in the back of his throat, licking his lips lustfully as he dove down onto his lover of the night's shaft, taking it deep into his mouth.

He moaned around it, on all fours, nose dipping, pressing his soft, flexible tongue up and around all of it that he could, learning how to use the new shape of it more appealingly. It was better than a human tongue, so very much better, but he had to learn how to use it, to sweep it around those soft barbs, more like nodules than anything that could have at all been considered sharp. He grunted thickly, wanting more, but Dale was blushing, thrusting up to him, the softer pads of his paws slipping on the smooth floor, not finding much grip amongst the lust of everything else.

But it didn't matter. In fact, nothing in the outside world mattered anymore, not as Gage experimented, nude but for the fur covering his half-human half-canine body, every bit his fursona, but, in a way, better too. He was still him, taking the best parts from Gage the man and Gage the anthro, slurping wetly down the length of that shaft, messy and drooling, but no one cared about a bit of mess. Not when there were much kinkier things to lean one's attention into, after all.

"Oh... Oh, damn... Damn... Gage?"

When he looked up, pulling back so just the rounded, soft tip of Dale's shaft was in his mouth, his tail could not help but to wag. There was such lust on Dale's face, whiskers quivering, lips parted, so cutely mewling, whimpering, tiny tremors going through his body. He could not resist it and the reverberations subtly moved up the feline's body. He bore his legs back a little, letting them splay out so that there was room for the dog anthro between them.

If they had not been surrounded already by lustful moans, whines and whimpers, there might have been more to the moment than that, a breathy pause with the tapered tip of Gage's cock pressed enticingly up to Dale's pucker. His arms hooked around the cat anthro's legs and the two of them knew it was too quick yet there was nothing else that could possibly have been more perfect, waiting there, breathing in, breathing out, though both wanting exactly the same thing.

Gage bore in slowly, letting his partner adjust to his size, though he was not oversized, simply perfect. That was where, of course, real life differed from rather a lot of furry art and fiction, though the real size was more than enough, the feline squirming in his arms, buttocks hitched up. Dale let out the cutest of mewls and meows as his backside was so very slowly and lovingly plundered, a hot length that he had not expected stretching him out and out, a growl on his lips.

"Ohhh, Gage!"

He was a different person, after all, as his fursona. A little sweeter, a little more inclined to squirm, blushing cutely, finding a part of himself that could only be expressed as his feline fursona. Yet that was part of the beauty of being furry in what was not possible in a mere human body, pushing and testing the limits of imagination in what could be, what would be.

With the taste of Dale's shaft and a hint of thickly tasting pre-cum in his mouth, the dog anthro thrust slowly, testing what he could take, how deep he could go. His partner cried out for him, the disco lights flashing over them yet again, squirming and writhing as if he wanted more, trying to grind onto his cock. Gage's tongue hung out as he panted, a dragon on all fours near them getting his ass rimmed, though the blue jay anthro on the other side seemed to be having a whale of a time as a horse anthro rode his shaft, head thrown back in open ecstasy. They were surrounded by such lust and openly kind debauchery that it was right to be where they were, Gage panting heavily, leaning over Dale, ensuring that there was as little space between them as possible as he thrust, long, slow strokes claiming the feline's anal passage there for the first time.

It felt different to any kind of anal sex he'd had before, wanting to thrust, falling prey to what he might have called feral need. His pink coat caught the hue of the lights, though his strong body would not be denied, muscle ever so lightly showing through a coat of fur that, honestly, was a little thicker than Gage had imagined it. But the Alsatian anthro was not about to complain about something like that as the silver tabby feline under him mewled and bucked, his cock standing up hard and proud, another drop of pre-cum drooling from it.

Feral need tingled through him, a burning flare that had his balls aching, now covered in a soft coat of fur, yet feeling just that little larger and fuller than they had as a mere human. Even the feeling of his sheath tugging and pulling ever so lightly around the base of his cock had him panting even more heavily, pushing on, finding a pace, thrusting, squeezing into that tight hole again and again. Dale's mewls drove him on, finding himself, who he was, the stripping down of sexual lust bringing them to a state of being that could not be achieved when people, let alone furries, were putting on a mask out in the real world.

There, with furries fucking all around them, making love, taking it rough or easing it gently, there were no limits, Dale clinging to his forearm, the other arm flung back behind his head. The feline tried to buck up against him, legs hanging more heavily over Gage's arms, but the dog was too far gone to stop unless he was asked, thrusting and grinding, something pulling deep inside.

He knew what he had to do before the moment even came to pass, the anthro pushing inside his partner, the tight fit that had already been present suddenly becoming even tighter, so much tighter. That canine bulge of his swelled as soon as he got close to climax, locking them together willingly, his body something like he remembered it to be but with so many more exciting new qualities that it was hard to keep track. But he was an anthro, moaning out his lust, thrusting into Dale's backside with short, sharp pumps, need rising, his cock aching, needing it more than ever, on the brink of losing control – all in the best of ways.

Yet it was Dale that climaxed first, scrambling for his shaft with a handpaw but not quite reaching it in time, cumming without his hands as short spurts of cum flowed forth. He wriggled and twisted, tail lashing under him, though it was nothing compared to the rapidly wagging tail of the Alsatian, thrusting harder, deeper, unable to pull back with how their bodies were stuck together.

Closer… He panted heavily, tongue fluttering with every snatch breath, eyes half-lidded. So close…

He climaxed with a howl, throat trembling, wanting to throw his head back but only making a strangled sound instead, grunting, whining, crying out Dale's name repeatedly. No one near reacted as he thrust and thrust, though not a drop escaped with the swelling of his shaft to ensure they stayed closely tied together. Dale moaned loudly, head falling back, fingers tight on Gage's arm, though he relaxed his grip after a moment, wriggling, teasing, squeezing down on the shaft up his backside, testing out the limits of his own, new body.

"Ohhh… That feels…different."

Gage grunted, struggling for words.

"Mmmph… How so?"

The feline whimpered, though the smile on his lips was back, green eyes dancing, full of mischief.

"It feels *right*."

And that was all that a moment like that needed to be, one orgasm following another for those around them, though the canine moved over Dale, letting his body rest as close to him as possible. He didn't want to put his weight on Dale at first, but the cat kissed his cheek and then his lips and told him how silly he was being.

"Like you think I can't take your weight!"

Of course, Gage was bigger and more muscled, though not heavily so, not in a way that Dale could not handle, the tabby cat wrapping his arms around him, stroking down his back, marvelling at the softness of his fur. So plush and light, it moved through his fingers easily, though Gage had more to give than that as he kissed the cat anthro deeply, tongues tangling, though there was only one of them, in such a sweet dynamic that fit together so perfectly, that could come out dominant.

Inside his backside, Gage's cock throbbed. Dale moaned. In those anthro forms, one round would not be enough. So it was that Gage thrust again, slowly, making love to the guy and the furry that he had only hoped that he might "have something with" before, all coming to light in a glorious way, even if no one could have said what had truly happened in the madness of transformation.

Furries would be tossed into bed with partners from all anthropomorphic species, bodies coming together in twos, threes, fours and even more. No limits were to be imposed where consent was given and those that had never quite fit into their bodies were brought into the light, passion flaring out with the blistering heat of a dragon's breath.

Alas, the night had to slip by and, with its passing, came the dawn, a softening of the transformative effect that brought them, slowly but surely, back to the human-furry bodies that they had entered the con with. Only in sleep did the changes reverse themselves, bringing back fursuits and apparel, though the ripped off T-shirts and fetish wear, in some cases, would be left where they'd been torn off in fits of passion.

Snuggled up in Dale's hotel room, however, two furries were very much where they wanted to be.

When they woke the next morning, transformed back to their human forms, they would remember, though not everyone would believe what had taken place there. The relationships formed in the kinky sway of public play and transformation, their dreams becoming a reality, however, would forever remain, Gage and Dale kissing goodbye outside the con, their rides waiting.

Soon, they would see each other again, Gage about to finish university, looking for a new city to move. With the kisses of his furry partner lingering on his lips, he grinned foolishly, for he had an awful lot to smile about all of a sudden. He'd been looking for a change anyway.

And, at the furry convention, he'd found an even bigger change than he had been expecting.

He couldn't wait for his next one!

Charming a Dragon

Tezzynth, known as Tezzy to his friends, ducked his head shyly, sitting on the edge of the lake with just his forepaws in the water. It was too hot to go out to the meadow or even down to the beach, although that offered the respite of the water too, finding that the ocean salt made his scales itch, so it wasn't something that he much wanted to combine with the brazen nature of the summer sun. His blue scales shimmered faintly, well-oiled and cared for, though his horns were still small, protruding only a little way from the back of his skull. His entire body was still light and delicate, a mature young adult even though dragons lived for many hundreds of years and he still had time to grow into the full entirety of his body.

"What's the matter, don't want to go in?"

His boyfriend, Braison, smirked and dipped his tail in the water, the spade-shaped tip swirling and swirling, toying with the idea of splashing his partner. Tezzy frowned, sticky and stiff in the heat, though it would still not have been something beyond Braison to, well, "poke the dragon" regardless of how Tezzy felt about it.

"Yes…" Tezzy said, dragging out the word. "In a bit. I'm just relaxing here. Sometimes we can have quiet too, you know, hon."

Braison sighed. With his dark scales, he didn't feel the heat as much, his body better-designed to absorb and allow it to dissipate, a dorsal-frill running down his body from the back of his skull to the mid-section of his tail. It cooled him a little as he funnelled the lightest breath of wind down the sides of his body as he pleased, though there was nothing Braison liked better than to lie, stretched out, in a cool patch of soil or even in the edge of the lake itself to cool off.

Yet the lure of the lake was there too and he stood, flicking his tail, inviting his lover in with the tall pines to bear witness to them, sunshine gleaming off his black scales.

"Dear... Come cool off with me," he murmured invitingly, tickling the tip of his tail up under Tezzy's chin. "You know you want to and you look so good under the water..."

Tezzy grumbled softly in the back of his throat, but it was merely a sound that came as he was pretending to hold back, dipping a toe in the water and then turning his head away. What Braison did not catch there, however, was the cheeky grin stretching his lips wide.

"Nope! Too cold!"

"Oh, come on!"

Sadly, Braison was not one to take to jokes like that all too easily and, being a little larger than Tezzy, he too easily knocked him into the lake with a well-placed swipe of his tail. In but a moment, a squeal and a flail later, the blue dragon was in the water, heaving and gasping, the pebbles dropping off sharply from where he had only been paddling before.

"Braison!"

But his lover only blew him a kiss, bringing a wing-tip to his lips instead of a paw, cheekiness gleaming in his eyes.

"If you want payback for that, you'll have to catch me first!"

And the game was on, the black drake sinking beneath the surface, kicking and twisting to fight against his natural buoyancy. The biggest problem for dragons when they wanted to swim was the fact that the air within them that helped them to fly wanted to drag them back to the surface constantly. Yet the forces of gravity were too always striving to drag them down in flight, so they were well-used to working against something that strove to push them back, building up the muscle and the fitness to fly either through the air or in water. Wings worked as well as fins and Braison shot deep, a stream of silvery bubbles flowing from his hide, tracing his path.

He always led and Tezzy knew he was a safe lover to follow, following the wisp of his tail-tip as he sank deeper and deeper. It was easier for Braison to swim than it was for Tezzy, but the blue dragon was still a more than competent swimmer as he swung his head back and forth, questing for something deeper, letting the cool of the lake wash over him. Away from the reaches of the sun, the water was colder, more patient, slipping over his scales and teasing the heat from his bones.

He sighed, bubbles streaming from his lips. That was just what he needed. Not that he was going to tell Braison, of course, that he'd been right, but some things just were right. The flow of water as he swam over the other dragon caressed his scales as if the other dragon was actively brushing up against him, though there was still distance between them. And it was that distance that was interesting in its own way, something that Tezzy ached to close, the cool of the water revealing something warmer that had been simmering beneath the surface all day.

Oh…

Without the blistering heat of the sunny day to distract him, Tezzy groaned, bubbles dotted along his shaft as it, very slowly, eased from the slit at the base of his belly, while he swam. It was slender, a probing sort of length, and he wriggled his hips back and forth a little, letting it come forth. The sensation of water brushing it was strange and yet something that he wanted to lean into, seeing perfectly even as the water grew a little murkier the deeper they both swam.

Maybe Braison was in the same predicament as him, away from the heat of the sun, but it was obvious to see when the other drake's pink, fleshy length was on its way out, thicker and meatier than Tezzy's. It quested for something even as Braison swam, flipping on his back to cast a cheeky grin back at his partner, even though it was more of a flirt than an open invitation. Tezzy shivered, water rippling around him. Despite being together for some months, taking it slow…they hadn't taken it *all the way* yet. But the taste of that cock was oh so very familiar to Tezzy and the dance of the dragons was not something he was ever about to turn down.

Dipping and swishing and swimming in and out of one another like fish, they twisted and turned and yet the heat of their lust for one another could not be escaped even beneath the surface. Tezzy's chest tightened, his body wanting to suck in a breath even though he was underwater and could not. He wanted to, oh, how he did… Yet the tingles of the lure of that first time, feeling that length inside him in a different way, made it so that he could not refuse the pleasure, not for himself, even after taking a while to get to know Braison and prepare himself for it.

He struck out for the surface, his partner hot in pursuit, their shafts dragging them back against the water, for they were not, by any means, the most aerodynamic body part to have out on show. Still, he sucked in a deep breath as water streamed from his muzzle in the open air, Braison joining him, but not even Braison could have expected Tezzy to capture his lips in such a passionately deep kiss.

"Mmmph…"

Tezzy sucked in a breath through his nostrils, the pucker and the flare of them tingling, tickling strangely. A strap droplet of water rolled down between the ridges of his eyes and he groaned into Braison's lips, a tilt of his muzzle allowing their tongues to tangle, winding together, the kiss deepening further. Without thinking, Braison rocked and ground his hips, his fat length sliding up against Tezzy's longer one, need rising, a flush of heat coming to the older dragon's cheeks as he broke away.

"Ah…" He chuckled, shaking his head as if to clear it. "Sorry about that, some things got on top of me there. How about we go back to shore and I'll see about making you cry out my name again, darling?"

Of course, he meant a little oral attention, the only thing that they had done before in a sexual endeavour, whimpering and winding together, learning about one another's bodies. Braison may have lost his virginity sweetly to another but that was still yet to come for Tezzy, the slightly younger dragon wanting to wait and see whether or not he was with the right one. Yet… He swallowed hard, licking his lips. Didn't he already have the answer to his question? His scales prickled with nervous tension, excitement leaping and turning in the pit of his stomach.

"I'm ready."

Braison started, eyes wide, though there was a look of hunger in the depths of them too.

"What – you mean, really? Now?"

Yet he did not swim away, only pressing in all the closer to Tezzy, scales brushing up against one another, tenderly sensual. Their cocks teased together as Tezzy clung to Braison, only managing to do so without whimpering with the heat of the sun cooled by the lake, their proximity to the water lightening and softening. It would have been too hot, far too hot, to do anything out of the water even if they had realised where their needs were to begin with. It was all happening at long last and need curled within Tezzy's heart as the water splashed up around them, streaming off their long necks, muzzles once again locked together in passion.

A kiss from a dragon could not be held forever, however, when there were other needs to meet and Braison was not the sort of drake to resist pleasing his partner. With a kiss and a purr, he dipped under the surface, his nose questing for the treat of Tezzy's cock, the light blue length the perfect size for his jaws.

As his lips folded carefully over his teeth and Braison took Tezzy's cock into his mouth, the dragon with his head still above the surface moaned, paddling, fanning his wings out across the surface of the water to help himself stay afloat a little longer. It was all he could do to stay there, afloat, head wanting to roll back, tongue hanging out, panting heavily as his maw hung open to release heat that he had not even known was in there. His tail acted as a balance, anchoring him in place, but he didn't have to worry about anything, not even moving, as Braison took care of him in the best way that any lover could.

"Ohhh…"

That long tongue of his wound its way sensually around Tezzy's cock, his lover knowing just what he liked, rippling and massaging in the strangest of ways, as slick and as wet as ever. Tezzy moaned aloud, shuddering bodily, but there was nothing he could do, not even at that moment, but accept all that the drake had to offer him, hips rocking and trying to hump even though he could not thrust very much. No, that would have been too much for him, in such a position, needing the calm, the coolness of the water sweeping and swirling and flowing around him. If he'd thrust into that sweet, sweet maw too, however, there was no telling just what lengths he would go to.

Tezzy's head drifted, the smooth suckle of his lover's maw around his cock all that he could think about. The tongue twitched and pulsed as if he was thrusting, though Tezzy didn't even quite know what thrusting was in sex as yet, how it would play out, whether he wanted and needed to feel the force of such passion flowing through him. It felt better, so far, to be on the bottom, sucking down Braison's cock, but he still wanted pleasure of his own too, everything coming together in a sweetly confusing manner.

Maybe that's just how it was meant to be for his first time. Either way, he knew he was safe and cared for with Braison, the one who had finally, through patience alone, got him to open up to the possibilities of the body. Tezzy loved him just a bit more for that, for there never had been any pressure, despite the difference in their levels of sexual experience. Maybe there needed to be more dragons like Braison in the world.

Yet he could not think, not as his head tried to roll, muscles tensing, his body not quite knowing what to do with itself. It was all that he wanted, lust getting the better of him, struggling even then to keep his head above the surface of the water. He gulped and down as much air as possible, moaning as his lover sucked down his cock, though the pleasure of being lusted after in turn too was something that he yearned for, ached for. He'd never considered having a partner like Braison before he'd met him but, after they had come together, he didn't know just why it had ever not been an option.

Braison didn't stop suckling down his cock, however, even knowing that his lover was struggling to contain everything. His throat worked, swallowing constantly even though it was only the very tip of his partner's cock that pushed up into the back of his throat. As a dragon, he didn't have a gag reflex, but it still felt better to keep his throat working, hungrily drawing Tezzy's cock in even deeper still. It was all that he needed too, the saltiness of his pre-cum slipping straight down his throat.

The drake groaned, bubbles streaming. The need to breathe grew and grew but he couldn't just not breathe forever, even though he wanted to stay down there until Tezzy was at the point of orgasm, oh no. That would come in other ways, their bodies winding up and together, but he was sure too that his lover could climax twice in short succession if he was really good about it. And he *wanted* Tezzy to be relaxed…

Braison rumbled softly, letting the ticklish vibrations from his tongue and lips travel down into Tezzy's cock. His partner bucked against him, need evident, and he pushed on eagerly, lusting for it all even as his lungs burned.

In Tezzy's mind, he was getting too much seductive pleasure at that moment in time to consider Braison's comfort, though the dragon was more than capable of ensuring that he was taken care of too in that regard. He could come up for air anytime he pleased but Tezzy could not as his head sank, the water closing above him. He would just have to hold his breath for a little while longer, sinking and twisting back and forth, the pump of his tail urgently helping him thrust his cock just a little more.

So close… He was so close that he could feel it, lungs trying to pump and pant, jaws hanging open. He could not breathe though, wanting it all, moaning through a stream of bubbles, the silvery flickers obscuring his vision even underwater. It was brief though, revealing the pushing, churning shape of his lover down below, encouraging him on to the explosive high.

Maybe it was Braison and maybe it was the lack of air that pushed him there, but all Tezzy knew was that at one moment he wanted to kick back for the surface and the next he was pulled down under his lack of buoyancy, orgasm exploding forth. He tried to groan but nothing came out, the sound locked in his throat as his cock ached and pulsed, sending stream after stream of thick cum straight down his partner's throat. It was all that Braison could do, even then, to keep up with it, for Tezzy was known for being a little on the virile side, spurting and shooting his load deeper and deeper. He gulped swiftly, throat working, pulsing, taking down every drop that was offered to him, for everything that he wanted to do for his partner was already within the tenacious grasp of his claws.

Tezzy's head spun, needing air, but it was only the thrust of his partner's tail that got him back to the surface and taking a breath, lungs working furiously for all that he needed. The dragon growled luxuriously as his partner gulped down every drop of his cum, somehow still keeping his cock lightly edged up into the back of his throat through it all.

"Oh… Ohhh…" Tezzy moaned. "Braison, too much… Ah… Too… Too sensitive."

Braison, thankfully, heard him, though he was still fully in control of himself at all times. His need was up, however, his cock throbbing, pulsing, aching for more. His need had not yet been satisfied and Tezzy nodded to him, a smile pulling at his lips, though he was still delirious with desire, the afterglow of his orgasm warming him through. It was the kind of warming, however, that left him cool, the soft simplicity of the water flowing over his scales easing off any edges of tension that may have remained.

His lover wound around him as Tezzy drifted, allowing Braison to lift him up, both of their heads above the surface of the water. Braison stayed on the bottom, his wings flared out across the barrier between the water and the air to keep them both supported, though his cock rose hard and thick, demanding attention that only Tezzy's tail hole, in that circumstance, could give.

"Relax," Braison purred. "You don't have to do anything, just relax and enjoy."

Tezzy nodded faintly, clinging to Braison even though they were quite evenly matched in size, his wings falling down.

"I'm ready."

And there could have been no better place to be in the whole wide world as Tezzy felt his tail hole spread for the very first time. It was slow and it was slick, Braison's shaft producing its own, natural lubrication bit by bit as he eased into his partner. Tezzy's weight pulled him back onto that cock with rippling insistence, his breath catching, the sense of fullness spreading through him, deeper and deeper – far deeper than that cock could actually penetrate. Yet the sensation was there, nonetheless, pushing against his inner walls, a strange feeling of being opened up without actually doing anything to orchestrate it for himself.

Moaning out loud, Tezzy tried to gulp down all the air he could, yet found himself as devoid as breath as he had been beneath the surface of the water. He had to know, had to see, whimpering softly, wanting it all. That cock wasn't even all the way inside him and there was so much pleasure left to find, his shaft remaining hard and wanton even though he had only just climaxed.

Braison smiled open-mouthed, his need clawing at his soul, though he could not yet rock and grind as he wanted to. No, that would come later, sometime later, once Tezzy had got used to his length, although they would have to swap sides and turns too at some point, Tezzy getting the top spot. But the deed was in the middle of being done and the tightness of that hole closing around him was all that he needed, all that he craved.

Huffing hotly, he shook his head, swimming backwards, the thrust and swipe of his tail enough to propel him across the surface, however lightly. That too was enough to thrust and rock gently, softly enough for the inexperienced Tezzy, the dragon who was very much no longer a virgin moaning out his name.

"Oh... Oh, Braison."

It was unconventional to have one's first time out in the lake, but Braison could not think of any better way for any of it to go, his need rising, fluttering up to the surface with driving certainty. There was no way for him to stop what he had started, only wishing that he could fold his wings around Tezzy and draw him in close, moaning in turn as that already tight hole closed down *hard* around him. It was exotic, hotter than any session he had ever had before, but maybe that was due to the blue dragon above him, how the sunshine glittered off his scales, making his heart pound in new and unusual ways.

Oh...

Maybe Braison had been waiting for the right one too, the right one who made everything worth it, even though he had enjoyed himself before. For a relationship had to come naturally and, even with his shaft buried under Tezzy's tail, he could never imagine ever again being with anyone else.

Tezzy grunted and groaned, his cock throbbing against Braison's stomach as he pressed down, wanting more, craving it all. His grip on the other dragon slipped as he eased down with a grunt, his tail hole strained around that slightly shorter yet thicker length as the natural bob of Braison's body gave him everything he needed. Braison hissed against him, rasping out a heady breath, head twisting, pressing his nose in close to Tezzy's, nuzzling and licking at his muzzle.

"I need you…" He huffed, eyes burning with an intensity that Tezzy had never seen before. "Can… May I?"

Tezzy didn't have to ask what Braison meant as he moaned out his agreement, grunting softly, the words catching in his throat even as he squeezed down even more tenaciously around that meat. He couldn't do anything but allow it to spend itself inside him, for he was not sure his body would allow him to back off from that cock now that he was so close, so close. Braison's shaft twitched and throbbed inside him, aching for more, surely drooling so much pre-cum that had nowhere else to go but deeper.

Braison had no reason to hold back, not then, grunting and rocking, the water splashing up, threatening to pull them under, but his orgasm was there and flowing forth in the blink of an eye. He groaned and snarled, snapping as he twisted, yet his orgasm pulsed forth in spurt after spurt, filling him up with a slick, creamy load of thick cum. The dragon growled, tail swinging, slapping the water, but he couldn't do anything but ride out his orgasm even as Tezzy's moans mounted, riding him too in such a position as he took every drop of cum that Braison had to offer.

On and on, the stream of cum flowed, a load that had been saved up seemingly especially for Tezzy. He didn't have to worry about anything when Tezzy was there, kissing him back, their tongues tangling lustfully, hastily, needs simmering forth with a tingling rasp of delight.

Even a long orgasm, however, had to come to an end at some point, the drake moaning softly as they floated, his cock softening only slowly within Tezzy's backdoor entrance. There was time yet, however, for the two lovers to come together, letting the heat dissipate from their bodies softly and smoothly, jaws hanging open for the lusty rasp of breath.

"Oh… Braison," Tezzy tried to say, though the words were thick in his throat, tongue sticking to the roof of his mouth as he tried to find a way to get them out. "That was… You were… Oh…"

Braison chuckled lightly, dropping a kiss on his lover's cheek, water droplets trickling down those brilliant scales. Yet something caught his attention, hard and thick against his stomach, Tezzy's shaft ready to go for another round. The drake smirked, tongue flickering out of his maw.

"Hm… You're still hard."

Licking his lips, Braison curled up under Tezzy, the tip of his tail twitching.

"I can help with that."

Shuddering, the only word on Tezzy's lips was what he'd wished he'd said so long ago.

"Yes…"

He never had to worry about that again.

Not with his sweet Braison around.

All Tied Up

Darion groaned, the horse leaning back on the bed, though his hands were securely cuffed to the metal headboard. He'd wondered at just why a dragon anthro had needed a metal bed specifically when he'd first got together with Eowin and, frankly, had considered it to be some method of fireproofing. A rather poor one, granted, considering all the flammable material still present in the dragon's otherwise fairly normal home, but it was the best idea he could come up with.

That was, until, they'd started getting into kinkier things in the bedroom. Then he'd realised exactly how that metal framed headboard was useful for tying his wrists too, or using handcuffs, or even sometimes hooking things on to that they wanted to use. The stallion had never been adventurous in the bedroom, but only because he hadn't really thought that kind of play mattered to him.

He appreciated it more, however, when Eowin showed him exactly what he looked like in a photo, all splayed out, his chest pushed up in a sensual arch, his grey hide darkened with sweat. His tail had fanned out to the side of his hips that time and his cock was left half-hard, spilling a deluge of cream over his belly, which glistened in the softly lit bedroom. There'd been a faint smile on his lips, lips parted, and his eyes were unfocused and hazy in the aftermath of orgasm. That time, Eowin had edged him for so long he'd thought he was going to lose his mind, though the mind-blowing climax that had come at the end of it all had been worth it ultimately.

And the dragon posed a striking figure too, muscular and defined when he stood over the stallion in any submissive form. It was comforting to be down on his knees before someone who could easily protect him, covering him with his body any time needed –

though the dragon maintained scenes easily. A few years older than Darion, he had a little more experience, so to speak.

Yet his red and orange scales reminded Darion of the fire that lay within his belly: that extra fire-making organ that dragons had. The name eluded him as he lay there, blinking softly up at his dominant partner, all to better take in his thick, rounded shoulders and the muscular cut to his thighs. A fire-burst pattern danced up the tops of his thighs to his hips, finally striking a separate T-shape across his back, which Darion enjoyed tracing with his blocky, chunkier nails, reminiscent of hooves. There was so much gentle differentiation in the shading of the dragon's scales that he could have spent all day adoring them.

Maybe that was why it was better for him to be tied up and submissive, all so Eowin could do exactly as he pleased with him. The dragon's tail swung lazily, tipped with an arrowhead-like point, and a line of spines, which the drake could flatten to his back whenever it pleased him, dotted down the full length of his spine, from between the smartly hewn horns on his head.

"Hm… What to do with my lovely pony tonight," Eowin mused, as if he didn't have any idea at all, really, of what he wanted to do with the equine. "You're as eager as ever."

"Mm, well, it's you…"

Darion mumbled the words, his darker grey mane spilling over his neck and partly fanning across the bed. He tugged at his bonds, where he was tied to the headboard and the footboard of the bed, though was only testing them, not really striving to get free. His cock throbbed, the tip flat and partially flared, though that was just how his cock rested naturally while it was hard. The flare itself would be absolutely spectacular as soon as he was permitted orgasm.

If he was allowed to cum. But Darion didn't think Eowin was going to restrict him from that, not that time.

His cock throbbed as if in agreement, a tenacious bead of pre-cum clinging to the tip.

"It would be a shame to let a nice, hard length like this go to waste," Eowin said silkily, his tongue dragging sensually against the side of his muzzle as he spoke. "Mmm... That's what you'd like, isn't it? For me to take leave of my senses and spend all night worshipping your cock?"

"Nngghhh... Uh, well..." Words did not leap easily to Darion's lips, the stallion's muzzle twitching and quivering. "Maybe?"

He offered his dragon partner a cheesy grin, though it wasn't about to get him out of the scene they'd planned for that night, of course not. It was never meant to, not as he wriggled in place, his hind legs splayed out, so he was presented in a star-like shape, all stretched out and ready to be used. It was not a position, however, that put him in a position where Eowin could easily toy with the fleshy pucker of his tail hole, which made him wonder just what it was the dragon wanted to do with him that night.

Not knowing the specifics was part of the excitement for him. They had a safe word, of course, but they'd taken things slow and gentle, all so they could see what worked for them both at their own pace.

"Oh, no... I have better things in store for you," Eowin said with a smile, half-lifting one of his wings from where he kept them tucked in against his back most of the time. "Stay still, colt, and wait for me."

Of course, Darion was hardly in any kind of position to do anything else as he quivered there, grunting. He tried to hold back his nickers even as the dragon trailed his short, blunt claws around his hips, stimulating flesh that was too sensitive to such a precise touch.

Yet Eowin produced a small toy, a little egg-shaped thing with a longer string of silicone attached to it – clearly for retrieval. With a slick coating of lube, it slipped up easily into the stallion's tail hole, though it was tricky to easily get at it with the horse's heavy nuts hanging over his soft doughnut. Darion grunted lightly, though the egg was easy enough to take; he had an inkling of just what it could be used for.

"Mmmph…"

"How are you feeling? Colour?" Eowin checked in with him.

"Uh…" Darion considered in, wriggling in place. "Green? But what is… Oh!"

The drake switched on the vibrating egg, letting it burst to life, though Darion would never know quite how Eowin was able to place things so precisely. For the egg was wedged exactly up against his prostate and he whinnied too shrilly, trying to buck and grind his hips, ears splaying out submissively in pleasure.

"Mmmph!"

"There you go, pony, that's quite a ride for you."

The dragon openly delighted in Darion's bonds, how he strained, muscles bunching and flexing. He wasn't really trying to break free, of course, but merely following the path of instinct, panting heavily as the horse's pink tongue lashed across his lips, slick and fleshy. It did not protrude as far as the dragon's would have done, but it was still a sight to be seen. And Eowin knew just how that tongue felt when it was cradling his cock, scooping sensually up against the underside.

"Mmmm…"

Darion didn't know what to say, lips parted even as he breathed in sharp puffs of air through his nostrils.

His tail tried to swish, though all he could do was grind up helplessly as Eowin played his fingers around his cock, teasing with the lure of release.

Yet that release was not to come, of course, not until the dragons said he could cum. The horse licked his lips again and tried to contain himself as Eowin teased his cock, folding his fingers around without letting the claws graze the stallion's sensitive flesh.

"Mmph…"

"That's it, pony," Eowin breathed, his voice barely above a raspy hiss. "Relax now… I've got you."

For that was the true treat of submission, at least to Darion. For him, it all came together in how he could let things go, in how he could forget things, letting it all come to pass moment by moment. Even as he ground his hips up, he leaned into the moment and allowed tension to ease from his shoulders, cock twitching and pulsing within the grip of Eowin's paw.

The dragon licked his lips, locking his gaze with Darion's. The stallion simply couldn't look away, even as he tried to stay still, glutes tensing while he strained. The lines of fiery tension lingering in his body were simply exquisite, muscles bulging, though the grey stallion was only moderately muscled. When it came to horses, he was on the slenderer side to most, though Eowin had never mentioned anything of that nature to him.

"Mmm… It feels…good…" Darion panted, playing into all the dragon enjoyed hearing from him, focusing as hard as he could. "Please… Please, don't stop."

"Oh, I do love it when you beg," the dragon said softly, his deep tone not requiring him to raise his voice in the slightest to ensure he was heard. "Do it again for me, pony. Let me hear how much you want it."

Darion twitched, his tail swishing. It took the stallion a few moments to realise that his own reaction was due to the vibrating egg being turned up another notch, pulsating against his prostate as if that was its singular intent in life. The stallion half-closed his eyes, his throat aching as he tried to speak.

"Unff..." Why did the dragon's paw have to feel as good as it did on his cock? "I... I want you go to faster, to make me cum all over myself."

"Mmm, that's something," Eowin said playfully, rubbing the flat of his thumb over the head of Darion's shaft. "Keep going."

The dragon didn't make it easy for him, playing with his length as he slid his paw down to the sheath, pushing it back a little more. The soft, velvety sheath pulled around the dragon's fingers, though Darion huffed as his nostrils flared, resting where he could, though meagre snatches of breath simply didn't simmer down the tension in his chest.

"I... I..." Oh, the words just wouldn't come! "I love having you over me...like this. I love being...on the bottom. I wish... I wish there were more ways I could say that."

Darion quivered. That wasn't something he'd been expecting to come from his lips in the slightest, though that was, by the nature of BDSM play, something that submission simply allowed him to bring to the forefront of his being. It was unexpected, yet the ropes allowed him a measure of vulnerability and security that were not usually felt.

The dragon smiled, allowing him a moment to feel his feelings, to understand exactly how that affected him. He groaned, nostrils fluttering, and Eowin gently brought him back to the moment, sliding his paw up and down.

For all his teasing about bringing the horse off time after time again that night, it was very tempting to do that. To make him cum so many times over that Darion was left a broken mess of a stallion, cream splattered over his abdomen and thighs as if he simply had not been able to control the spray of his cum.

But that was not where release lay for the stallion that day, not as his cock throbbed within the clasp of Eowin's paw. The stallion grunted, working his jaw slightly, though Eowin had all the words he wanted from him.

"Relax, breathe."

Darion huffed, welcoming the instruction. His head was pleasantly spacey and he didn't quite know what he was doing in the moment, though it was not all that bad. He was safe there, even if his body ached for orgasm increasingly, every pump of the dragon's paw bringing him closer. And yet the drake didn't take him over the edge as his flare engorged, swollen and throbbing with every beat of his heart.

"Mmmph... Please..."

He whimpered, mouthing words, though the stallion could not be sure whether he actually verbalised them. It ceased to matter in the moment, tied up right where he wanted to be, biceps and triceps bulging as his body, unwittingly, fought his bondage. Yet the mere act of straining against the ropes once again reminded him that he couldn't get free and, ultimately, he was secure in its hold.

That was all he needed, exhaling in a sharp puff of air as the buzz of the vibrating egg ramped up again, though he was not quite allowed over the edge of orgasm. Eowin seemed to know exactly when to pause or simply slow the pump of his paw, his fingers moulding seamlessly over the medial ring. It was something, after all, the dragon had toyed with many, many times before.

If he didn't know Darion's body, whoever would?

"There you go, pony," he breathed, calming the air as the horse twisted lightly, his eyelashes beading very faintly with drops of moisture. "It's coming... But you will earn it simply by looking pretty for me first. No more is needed, truly, trust me."

Darion had to trust him, though Eowin would never lead him astray, he was sure of it. The dragon had held him fast in every session so far and their time outside the bedroom was every bit the relationship Darion had wanted for a long time.

Even in the ties of bondage, secrets could be released, a sore part of the stallion's heart healing, locking back into its rightful place.

The passion of need flowed through him, however, and Darion could not so easily set it aside as if it had never been as he hungered for orgasm. He drooled lightly, a gleam of saliva marking the corner of his lips, though the stallion didn't notice it beyond a light flicker of sensation. Grunting, he swallowed a neigh, not wanting to give too much of himself away too swiftly, yet Darion was not in control of himself enough for that to ever be the case.

He whinnied, pulling the sound into an embarrassingly high pitch. Torn between grinding down against the vibrating egg and humping up into the lure of Eowin's paw, the stallion found himself caught in a truly delicious place. Wherever he turned there was a new sensation to enjoy. From the pull of the bedsheets under his back to the dampness of sweat cooling on his hide and, of course, the tighter grip of the dragon's paw sliding smoothly over his flesh.

That was where his mind focused, finding solace in the more rhythmic pump. Yet he was permitted beyond that edge, heat pooling in the turgid line of his shaft, the flare pumping up thick and full with every stroke.

"Ah… Ah!" He all but yelped, throat tight with need, grinding his hips up with all the force he could muster. "What… Eowin!"

"Come on, pony," Eowin coaxed. "It's just the one and you'll be down on your knees for me, as sweet as ever, the rest of the night. I see you need this."

Words were left unspoken in lieu of pleasure as Darion nickered throatily and gave himself over to the moment – just as his dominant wanted him to. There was no reason at all to hold back and he panted heavily, his chest rising and falling sharply with every snatched breath he dragged into his lungs.

Everything seemed to play out in slow-motion, at least for some moments, heat flooding his cock in the seconds immediately preceding orgasm. His cock pumped up thickly, the flare quivering with the strained extent it was engorged, fit to burst. Yet it only heralded the flow of cum to spurt from him, his balls aching as if they were being pinched and squeezed within a much larger hand.

Yet he was just there to ride out the moment and allow his dominant to take him there, thrust after thrust, even if it was just Darion imagining the act of thrusting. The stallion lost sense of himself in the moment as he let out a whinny that didn't sound very much like a stallion, cutting blisteringly through the air, the dragon taking him just where he needed to go.

Then and only then did the beauty of orgasm wash over him: an unstoppable flood that roared through his body, sweeping the horse up and away. Eowin leaned on to his lower abdomen, grounding him, the stallion's buttocks pressed into the bed, indenting it, while arc after arc of cum spurted from the head of his cock. His flare pumped, shuddering with every release, and it shot over his belly, halfway up his chest too, leaving glistening trails of cum in sensual arcs across his grey hide.

There was no way to conceal his lust, even as the dragon carried him through every moment of it, for it was not Darion's to take. With Eowin, if he'd thrown everything they'd built out the window, it would have felt more akin to stealing it. And he didn't want that, no, not at all.

He just wanted to be there, finding comfort in sucking Eowin's cock, taking the dragon's ridged dick right up into the back of his throat, all in thanks for allowing him the space to be himself, who he truly was. It was rarely found those days and the stallion collapsed back to the bed with his chest heaving and vision clearing, a smile pulling insistently at his lips.

"Ah, I see you're back with us," Eowin joked, climbing up on to the bed and checking the horse over. "All good? How are you feeling?"

He meant to investigate deeper into how Darion was but the look in the stallion's eyes gave him pause. Darion's eyes locked on to his cock, as if he wasn't even able to look the drake in the eyes at that moment, grunting softly as his tail swished.

"Green," he croaked, clearly in need of water but not wanting it at that moment. "Definitely green. Please… Sir. I need… I need…your cock."

He forced the words out with a blush searing across his cheeks and Eowin let out a tiny sigh, heart swelling with admiration for Darion, for how far he'd come.

"Of course, my lovely colt."

They'd discuss the scene later, what they liked and didn't like, but both consented to continue in the moment. Kneeling up and straddling the horse's chest, the dragon gave Darion exactly what he wanted and fed him the head of his throbbing cock.

Together, they really could surpass all bonds.

Strangers in Vegas

Las Vegas was loud and brash, flashy lights and cars stark around every street corner. Fashions that would have not had a place anywhere else in the world ran amok, the scene and the time for rash decisions. Many a fur had got hitched in a flurry of drunk mishaps, waking up the next morning with a cheap ring on their finger whether they were male, female or no longer sure after the events of the night. It was the lure of a city where anything could happen and one would always leave with a new story to tell for years to come. Everywhere a fur travelled through the neon and concrete, life bustled, the city never resting.

And Pax hated every second.

Sprawled on the king-sized bed of his empty hotel room, the palomino equine sighed, his broad chest deflating. On the other side of the wall, the clamour of his parents readying themselves for a night out with Sera, his sister having returned from university for the family holiday, echoed through. Pax groaned and rolled on to his cream-coloured front, shoving his muzzle beneath the pillows. He was due to attend university in the fall, like his sister, but he'd taken a gap year. It would help a great deal if he knew what on earth he wanted to do.

The door creaked open and he flicked his tail, the white hairs silken. The other fur closed the door quietly and waited for him to speak, patiently quiet for a minute that stretched into an age. Pax tensed, the muscles in his bare back – for he'd forgone any clothing other than jogging bottoms – tensing.

Go away, go away, go away, go away...

"You sure you don't want to come, bro?"

The mare's lilting tone was unmistakable and Pax nipped his lip, glancing back over his shoulder as light filtered into his dark crevice beneath the pillow. It felt safer there than in the rat race of the outside world, too changeable to keep pace with. Why couldn't his sister leave him in peace? He swallowed a sigh.

"Nah…"

The mare padded over to the bed, her larger hooves quiet on the thick, plush carpet, and perched on the edge, resting her hand in the centre of his back. Though muscles quivered, he remained still as she stroked down his spine with neat but distinctly more hoof-like fingertips, easing the tension from his body. Slowly, stroke by stroke, he relaxed into his sister's touch and pressed his muzzle into the bed, letting loose a soft nicker. She chuckled and played her fingers down to the small of his back, pausing to massage the spot above his tail. That was still okay with him, yet the stallion shrank into the bed a little more, close to his limit already.

"You didn't get ready in here?"

It wasn't much of a question, but it was all Pax had for her, keeping up appearances so that she would not ask him any more questions. She would not nose if she talked about herself, that much he knew.

"Oh…" She teased her fingers through his mane, softly companionable in a sisterly manner. "Yeah, mum and I were helping each other get the zippers on our dresses up. I can't twist to do it myself."

She chuckled.

"Kind of silly really."

Pulling his muzzle out from the pillows, he blinked up at the familiar brown muzzle with the white stripe. Her blue eyes smiled at him, black mane neatly oiled and braided along the arch of her neck. She was more of a traditional, heavy-set cob than he was, skin taut over muscle and weight she carried well. Most would call her curvy, or thick. He had called her far worse as a younger, crasser colt.

"It's not silly," he said. "You don't have the flexibility to reach back. But I could have helped if you'd asked."

"Why?" Her eyes brightened. "Did you want me to daub eye shadow on you too? You'd look so *pretty* for all the hot mares out there!"

He grunted and rolled his eyes, avoiding the bait. He had only been caught with his mother's make-up *once* when he was very young and he didn't think he would ever hear the end of the story. It would go on and on and on and on until it was finally told at his wedding day, or so he had been playfully threatened. He didn't doubt that his family would pounce on the opportunity to embarrass him, but he didn't think that he would have a wedding either, not with how he was as a stallion.

Pax shook himself. There was no time for those thoughts.

Sitting up, he looked his sister over, momentarily blinded by the sparkles on her dress. The little red number had more sequins than fabric and he stifled a snort, clapping a hand over his muzzle a moment too late. The mare sat back, painted red lips twisting as she tilted her head, her brother's eyes too wide and innocent to be believed.

"What?"

Sera frowned, crossing her arms over her breasts and thankfully hiding her plunging bosom. Slowly, so as not to lose control and burst into giggles, Pax swung his legs over the edge of the bed as his sister rose to take a step back, eyes sharp.

"Don't you think you want to...I don't know..." Pax tried to be tactful. "Go for something a little less...loud?"

She wrinkled her muzzle, ears twitching.

"What are you trying to say, little brother?"

He flinched. He hated when she called him that, yet Sera insisted. It was better not to make a scene, even though she was only one year older than him. Sera was formidable to say the very least of her attitude. And colts were liable to become tongue tied, hoof-in-mouth disease a common problem amongst his kind. Pax swallowed hard and brushed his forelock out of his eyes, long lashes catching on the soft strands of hair.

"Nothing at all," he said, lips curved into a smile, the picture of innocence. "But you look beautiful tonight. Only the best stallion could match you and give you what you deserve."

Though heat flushed her cheeks, the mare looked away, rubbing her forearm in a distracting motion. Embarrassment, however, did not suit her features well and the sly gleam in her eye swiftly returned, a hand on her hip as she jutted it out cockily.

"Well, my taste leans more towards felines lately." She grinned and brought her finger to her lips in a "shush" gesture. "Something about the claws... They feel fantastic when they prick into my –"

"*Sera!*"

Pax shot to his hooves, holding his hands up and shaking his head hard enough for his neck to hurt. If he had been younger, he would have held his hands over his ears and mumbled nonsense so as not to be forced to hear of his sister's exploits. Sera could be graphic at the best of times and he didn't want to know what she would say with the aroma of her first Long Island of the night on her breath.

"Don't sound so shocked, little brother," Sera laughed. "Maybe we'll find you a nice lady yet. She doesn't have to be a horse, no matter what mom and dad say. Species doesn't matter as much as they say and the world is changing..."

Her eyes grew distant and she stared over his shoulder. The mare tucked an imaginary strand of hair behind her ear, even though her mane didn't have a hair out of place.

"I mean…" Words spilled forth. "What does species matter, really, when you think about it? I mean, really think about it. We're all furs, aren't we? We're evolved, grown, better than our ancestors were. Why should it matter who we choose to spend our lives with when the curtains close?" She closed her eyes. "At the end of the day?"

Pax twitched, tail flicking against the bed as he stood and stretched his arms above his head. Sera's ramble was not meant for his ears, yet he let her continue anyway, working out the idea in her head. He was not the one that anyone had to worry about ending up with another fur, but that was an issue for Sera to work through herself, if his suspicions were correct as to who had actually caught her eye b ack home. Nothing for a brother to pry into, unless his opinion was desired. And Sera had never wanted that before.

The stallion touched his sister's arm, halting her stream of vocalised thought, and nickered, bumping his nose into her cheek. She trembled, eyes glazed with the sheen of tears. The stallion's jaw clenched. That cat, whoever he was, better treat her right. Or else there'd be hell to pay from the so-called little brother himself.

"Whatever you choose, it shouldn't matter to anyone else," he said, feeling older than his years. "Mother and father won't mind who you're with, you know. You're the trial run, after all."

His eyes glinted.

"You know. As you're the oldest. They get to make all their mistakes on you."

"Why – you!"

Sera thumped him, though she only partially meant it. Swatting at her brother, she threw her hands in the air and huffed, half-turning away from the stallion with a sullen flick to her tail. For a moment, Pax almost felt bad. Almost.

"Come on, Sera," Pax said, sidling closer. "You know I don't mean it. Just trying to cheer you up. It was a joke, silly. Stop sulking. Please? For me? For your *little brother*?"

He pouted, lips pushed out and trembling false from his muzzle, the image of a scorned colt. It didn't take much for her to come around and she joined him in chuckling, bosom trembling with amusement. The stress melted from her shoulders and Sera giggled, a lock of hair falling loose from its braid into her eye.

"You're an idiot, you know that?"

She looked her brother up and down with perfectly made-up eyes, mascara curling and spreading her lashes delightfully. The mare cocked an eyebrow, lips twisting into a half-smile that did not rise on the other side of her muzzle. She blew her brother a kiss and spread her arms wide, fingers curling in to beckon him closer. He shook his head, but it was already too late as she forced him into the hug.

"Still short," she teased, drawing him in tight, chin tucked on top of his head. "When are you going to hit your growth spurt, hey, little brother? Surely you're due for it by now?"

"I've already hit it," he grumbled, squirming as he strove to escape her iron grip. "Bloody lay off, would you? You know I don't *like* this, Sera – let *go*."

She stepped back, ears slanted to the sides. Her expression flickered and he caught the briefest flash of hurt painting her face carefully cool, her smile not reaching her eyes.

"Well…okay then," Sera said levelly. "I'm sorry. I didn't mean to upset you. Just was teasing."

She shrugged, smile fixed. Turning for the door, she made as if to leave without another word. The spring vanished from her step and Pax stood with his hands held awkwardly at his sides, frozen in place until shock kicked his numb mind into action. He launched forward, scrabbling after her and tripping over his own hooves. He flung out his hand, his sister too far away already, just like she'd always been.

"Wait – Sera! Please! Hold on a second!"

Pausing at the door, she half-glanced back, tail swishing sadly. Her lipstick had smudged on to her perfectly white teeth.

"Maybe one day you won't push us away so," she said. "I don't mean to trap you in a hug…but maybe there's another way I can show I care for my brother. I just don't know. Jokes aren't so bad either. You used to joke with me before, so much."

Sera sighed.

"I'm sorry you don't like to be close to me. Pushed you too far. I know you don't mean it. Not really."

Pax stared dumbly at her. It was just a hug he'd turned down – was that so serious? How could someone take that so badly? Pax gulped, misunderstanding her perception of the situation. Who wanted to be clamped to their sister's breasts? He didn't like breasts! Was that so weird, regardless of anything? Of course not! He fumbled for words, tongue tied. The stallion growled mentally, his ears flat against his skull.

"I   don't   want   to   push   you away…but…wait…Sera?"

Pax shook his head as the mare disappeared, closing the door without another word. And, just like that, the room was once again empty but for the sound of his own breathing. Her hooves faded down the hallway, the mare gone.

The stallion rubbed the back of his hand, shock melting into stomach-churning upset. Spine-chilling sadness flooded him to the tips of his fingers, as if he had been plunged into a black pit.

The stallion scrunched up his muzzle, fighting down emotion. He was stronger than that. He was supposed to be stronger. He shouldn't feel sad. He should be running after his sister, finding out what exactly was wrong. He should be apologising.

Should, should, should: he hated that word.

The stallion pressed his hands over his muzzle, rubbing his knuckles into the sockets of his eyes. Why were things so complicated? Was there any understandable reason? He had not meant to hurt her. It was half her fault, though Sera had always said she was not to blame. Pax gritted his teeth. Would no one consider his feelings?

Anger flared, licking through his veins with an old, familiar heat. The stallion's back stiffened and he curled his hands into fists, containing it as it built, second by agonising second.

And then he snapped, teeth clicking physically together as if he had become a feral equine, losing himself to baser instincts. What the fuck did she think he had done wrong? He'd never liked anyone clinging to him – it was annoying! Even before! Why did she think that was going to change? Why did it matter to anyone? It was his fucking thing to deal with how he wanted!

He stomped, bringing his hooves down on the carpet with undue force and gouging strips of material from the base layer. Kicking over the chair beside the small desk, he slammed his palms into the wall, beating the same spot until the heels of his hands throbbed with pain and breath came in heaving, crazed gasps.

Sera. It was all because of *Sera.* She picked on everything and took everything personally. He'd helped her! He'd cheered her up again! And what had she done? Thrown a hissy fit because he didn't want to cuddle up like a lovebug! He pressed his forehead to the wall, snorting moist breath over the neutral cream paint. It was all the same, complaints and tantrums over nothing… Like all the other fucking times! Didn't she know she already had it made? So why did she have to stick her nose into his life?

He wheeled about, the whites of his eyes showing as he took stock of his anger, nostrils flaring. He knew he was going too far. Yet he was too far gone to turn back. The stallion snarled a curse to the empty room and launched a kick that threw him off balance, adding fuel to the fire.

Why did she get to have her whole life worked out for her? Sera had known for, like, forever what she'd wanted to do! Excelling in the sciences, she had always known that she wanted to work in medicine and was well on her way to becoming a doctor – one of the best, if her confidence in her exam scores was to be believed. And he did believe her, even if he did not want to. She was Sera. She was his sister. She had everything worked out.

And he didn't. Not one bit. While she hated who he was. The sister he just wanted a shard of approval from, as sharp as it could be.

The anger seeped away as if through a drain in the floor beneath his hooves. His tail flattened to his rump as if for protection, though against what he did not know.

Pax stood in the centre of the room, chest heaving and sweat darkening patches on his golden coat. His back was sticky. He rolled his shoulders but only found a twinge in his chest. It was wrong to go off on Sera so much, yet he felt too much had happened for him to make peace with her. Stuff that she had no idea about, not in its true form, though still tackled clumsily. She had to stick her nose in. Even if she wanted him to be better, at her heart, she wanted to change him.

Pax sighed, exhausted now that anger had deserted, muscles trembling as if pushed upon by an exterior force. He unclenched his hand slowly, watching tendons move beneath the thinner coat of hair, clipped close to the skin. Every bone in his body ached, pain thrumming too deep for it to ever be massaged out with the gentlest caresses his mind could dream up. That was why he did not touch. Touch came harshly. And yet there was no one that could understand that.

He closed his eyes. Some pain was buried too far down for it to be dug up. He was yet to find good reason to look back.

Pax's eyes snapped open as he straightened, the natural curve returning to his spine. Standing around would do no good! At least he had not shouted at Sera. He could be proud of himself for keeping his head until then. And there was no sense in making himself feel worse. There was only one place that helped when he felt like this.

Muscles aching as if in anticipation, dug around the pale, wooden wardrobe for his battered gym bag. His parents, bless them, had said it was silly to take a gym bag on holiday, but he had known he would need it. The palomino equine licked his lips and fished out the black and yellow backpack, checking that his gloves were safely tucked inside.

It wasn't obsession that drove him to the gym. He inhaled deeply. The gym was not silly and neither was it vain, as others claimed.

It was his safety net.

*

Flat on his back on a bench in a half-rack and below loaded barbell, Pax huffed, panting for breath lost in the expenditure of energy. His black vest clung to his cut chest, muscle swelling proudly, and his hands hung down to the padded floor on either side of the bench. He put an arch into his back, easing out the strain after completing the last bench press repetition. The pain was a good pain.

Lucky this hotel has a reasonably well-equipped gym, he thought, casting around the wall-to-wall matting, suitable for heavy lifting. For a one-off expense, it would have set the hotel back, but Las Vegas was a place where extravagance reigned. So, it was good that lavish spending extended to the gym as he preferred to spend most of his time in one.

He curled his fingers around the cool metal, the bar weight twenty kilos when unloaded, and tensed his muscles expectantly. Pax paused and sniffed, his muzzle wrinkling in distaste. His gloves were starting to stink again. Pax smirked at the fleeting thought of shoving them in Sera's gaping muzzle later. That would be a brotherly thing, an acceptable thing, to show her, to teach her a lesson no one would raise an eyebrow at. Neither of them had batted an eye at roughhousing and the like, but digging into his feelings and being all soft with each other... To say the least, it wasn't for them.

He pushed the bar from the hooks and took the weight on his hands, arms shivering as if they would collapse under the weight of the plates slotted neatly on to either end of the bar. Bending his elbows, he pushed his chest up and brought the bar down to graze his chest, muzzle contorting. He strained, grunted, and made it rise, a push up to the top that raked breath through his lungs, muscles burning. It was an addictive sensation. Completing one rep, he did it repeatedly, driving the bar up with the cleanest form he could muster until eight repetitions had been squeezed from his tired body.

There was only one other in the gym and, in the middle of his set, Pax's skin tingled. Forcing himself to complete the set without interruption, he re-racked the bar and sat up, head spinning; it took a lot of effort to push his body past its limit. He looked straight into the eyes of another equine beside the long rack of dumbbells, a male more heavily muscled than he was. The black horse with a thick, black mane and tail blinked, startling green eyes fixed on Pax. He held a dumbbell in each hand, though was not close enough for Pax to tell how heavy each of them was.

Pax tried not to stare, but, if the other fur was going to be rude, he saw no reason to maintain his manners. Pushing his hands out from his chest, he worked out the soreness from his triceps: they needed a lot more work than he had time to give them. He did not rub the ache in his chest, however, thinking it would be strange to do it when another was staring directly at him.

The black stallion replaced his pair of dumbbells on the long rack. Pax huffed and brushed his forelock from his eyes.

Oh, *fuck*, he was coming over!

Playing it cool – he hadn't been giving him the eye, not really, he hadn't! – Pax rubbed his arm, wishing belatedly that he had something other than a vest top on. It was an overly showy look for gym-goers, but he'd reckoned, hey, he could get away with it on holiday. Now he wished he'd gone for his usual scruffy shirt, a lot less embarrassing.

Pax fidgeted as the horse approached, eyes bright. The stallion swallowed. How was it possible to have eyes that blue? He was probably another vain stallion who thought he was a stud and wore contacts to make the mares swoon. That thing about "piercing blue eyes" and all that jazz. Pax snorted.

"You're looking pretty good there," the stallion offered, stopping a respectful distance away. "Nice form."

Pax's ears pricked and he leaned forward, grabbing his water bottle with one hand. Buying time, he took a drink, water dribbling down his chin.

"I thought it was an unspoken rule of the gym not to interact," Pax commented dryly when he had thought of what he deemed to be a good enough response for the moment.

Water dripped off the equine whiskers on his chin and his lips twitched in imitation of a scowl. The damn things needed trimming again and itched something awful. The black horse chuckled and shook his head, blue eyes sharp with something unknown that set Pax on edge, heart racing.

"I suppose so," he conceded. "But it's quiet enough and you couldn't claim that this is a strict training gym. Rules are different here, or so I'll say myself."

Pax scratched his neck, considering.

"It's well enough equipped for training," he said, gaze sweeping the room. "Not just filled with cardio machines. No full power cage, but I'm grateful for whatever I get in hotels."

"Well equipped? You think so?" The horse's ears twitched and his forelock fell over one eye. "Thanks. I'm kind of responsible for that."

Pax leaned back, uncomfortable with how the other horse towered over him, though was not comfortable enough to stand either. He warranted that the equine was a good head taller than him, draft blood clearly rife.

"How are you responsible?"

"I work here," he answered simply. "Got the boss to put in better equipment." He laughed, a full-throated rumble. "Could you believe they had little pink dumbbells in here before? What good are those for anyone?"

His laugh was infectious and, unconsciously, Pax chuckled along, tail flicking against the bench. Taking a step to the side, the horse leaned on Pax's half-rack, taking the weight off one hoof.

"Small dumbbells aren't that bad," Pax said once the chuckles subsided. "Good for drop sets, burnouts or stuff like that... Light weight really kills for some lifts."

The black horse nodded, a fresh glimmer of respect in his eyes.

"What's your name then?"

"Pax." Pax held out his hand. "Good to meet you."

Shaking his hand in a firm grip, the stallion eyed him levelly.

"Pax..." He repeated the name. "I'm Diego. And the pleasure is all mine, believe me."

Pax released Diego's hand, fingers brushing as they separated. It was strange how, for males, physical contact was restricted. Anything more than a one-armed hug, handshake or slap on the shoulder was reason to cough in quiet discomfort. For a stallion disliking physical contact at the best of times, a handshake was about the most he could manage without flinching away, laughing to treat his retreat as a jest. He had the routine perfected for those who did not know him closely. Contact was to be limited.

So why did his heart abnormally, kind of fervently? His fingers tingled as if struck by a static shock; he curled and uncurled them to make the sensation disappear. He ran his fingers through his mane, an awkward silence falling between the two stallions, and swallowed.

Diego coughed into his hand, a long forelock half-covering his muzzle. Pax wondered how the stallion kept it so lengthy without it winding him up every second of every waking hour.

The stallion regained his wandering attention with a swish of his tail that sent the strands flying in a smooth, hypnotic arc.

"So…" Diego scratched behind his ear. "I've pestered you for long enough. I'd best let you get back to your workout. If you need any help, give me a shout, all right?"

He smiled. "After all, I am a trainer. That's what I'm here for, if you fancy it."

Pax nodded, something that he could not explain sending a twinge through his chest. The horse was good company, even in their short time chatting. He made Pax relax, muscles unknotting in a sensation that was both relieving and eerily foreign.

"Yeah…sure. I'll give you a shout."

With a flick of his tail, Diego made his way back to the other side of the gym, pausing for a split second to check his reflection in the mirrors stretching the length of the room. Hiding his smile, Pax let his body fall back on the bench, shoulder blades absorbing the impact as he raised his hands to the bar. It was suddenly a very lonely bar, despite being loaded with the same style plates that he always used. Across the gym, Diego grunted, working his way through a set of something Pax couldn't quite catch from his position. Pax snorted at the bar. Maybe the horse would come back over in some time. Chit-chat was not *that* much of a faux pas.

Or, if it was, he could make an exception. For a *Diego*.

He narrowed his eyes, focusing on the bar as he took the weight and brought it down to his chest so that he could not think of a silly horse with whom he had exchanged a few words. Arms burning, Pax glared the bar up, working through the repetitions with unrivalled dedication. It helped, soothing his mind, if but for a time.

When Pax came up from his final set, he raised an eyebrow at what the strange equine had clasped in his hand, eyes returning unwaveringly to Diego. While most carried a notebook to the gym or logged exercise on their mobile phone, he had a pack of playing cards in his pocket. Diego selected seven cards from the deck and flipped them over simultaneously. Choosing one, Diego nodded, laid it face-up on the end of a bench and selected dumbbells from the larger end of the rack. With a set of weights that would have made Pax's muscles scream and fail, the stallion hung his arms down to his sides and lifted his shoulders in a shrug, working the traps across his upper back. His muzzle twisted in a grimace and Pax stifled a chuckle. He was just as bad for making faces during that exercise.

Pax licked his lips as his mouth abruptly ran dry. He could not hold a handle to the weight Diego was using and doubted he ever would. He simply did not seem to be built for pushing and pulling heavier loads with his upper body, carrying greater strength in his legs. It was a shame when most males focused on the upper body, the chest and biceps. He wanted to match up with them too. He wanted other guys to look at him in the same way he looked at them. Pax exhaled, pressing his fingers between his eyes. A headache was well on its way.

Maybe, however... The horse pondered, ignoring the background grunts and huffs. Maybe the stallion had something good in his training regime that he could share with Pax? Something to break his plateau and push him further? He was a trainer and more experienced while Pax rarely had any assistance when it came to the gym. The equine learned as he went along, using all the videos and free help he could find, as privately as he could find it. Personal training was an unaffordable luxury to a colt on the edge of emptying his bank account even further for his studies.

He shouldn't interrupt someone in the gym, he had said so himself. Diego probably didn't even want to talk to a gangly colt. He was in a completely different league, ripped with only the tiniest sliver of bulk-gut showing through his grey t-shirt. The stallion stood to unload the bar while he considered the idea of requesting help, a foreign notion to his solitary mind. It didn't seem to make sense in his head, logic twisting so far that he could not recognise fact from fiction.

With the plates stored safely on the rack, Pax clapped his hands on his thighs. He could do it. It wasn't as if he would ever see the stallion again. So, fuck logic. Fuck whatever he thought. Where was the harm in talking?

Stifling nerves, Pax carted his gym bag to the other side of the gym, approaching Diego at a brisk clip of a walk. His blonde mane clung to his crest, strands soaked with sweat, and he arched his neck, petal-shaped ears pricked to the grunts of a stallion working hard. Finishing his set, Diego dropped the weights carefully on the matted floor and flexed his fingers to work out soreness. Pax sympathised with his pain.

"Hey."

Diego started, shuddering back for a fraction of a second in surprise. Pax grinned and chuckled, nostrils trembling as his mirth melded into an equine whinny of pure amusement. Diego joined him, rubbing his palms together, and dug out his pack of cards, gaze raised expectantly to the palomino.

"What's up?"

"Wondering what you've got there…and it's quiet enough to be a pest today and ask." Pax justified himself aloud. "Is that a routine you follow? How does it work?"

"I think you'll find that I was the one being a pest," Diego said, flashing Pax a set of startlingly white teeth. "But this is something like…hm… How much time have you spent in Vegas? Do you know what the game *Lucky Sevens* is?"

"*Lucky Sevens*?" Pax tilted his head to one side. "Yes, but those are different – curls. Three sets of each the upper, lower and full motion for a bicep. I worked them in not too long ago."

Diego half-shrugged and flipped the red backs of the cards over to reveal the face detail.

"I know of them but haven't used them in a while. No, this routine is like the game."

Pax studied the cards, each listing a different exercise in neat font with a number in the top right corner. The equine's brow furrowed.

"So…how exactly do you use these?"

Diego thumbed over the cards, sleek paper worn and curling in the corners of some if not most.

"It's simple. Like the game *Lucky Sevens*, you have to draw your selection of coasters or cards here – shuffled, of course – and flip them over. The one with the highest number, or difficulty rating, is the exercise you have to complete."

He tapped his fingers across the cards and drew one to demonstrate.

"This bench press card has a score of eight, but the card for leg curls scores one. If these were my choices, bench press would win."

"But that looks like…" Pax paused, looking over the cards. "All the harder exercises have higher scores against them, the compound movements. Wouldn't that make a workout very difficult? And full body?"

The stallion nodded, ears twitching as if he was pleased that Pax had caught on so swiftly.

"Yeah, it's meant to be difficult, one to make me think and work every muscle, not just in lifts. I find some yoga and Pilates things a dick to get done too. It's designed for a long, hard session," he said with a coltish grin. "Just like certain other activities…"

Pax raised an eyebrow yet made no comment. He'd been told that he had a dirty mind – by Sera – and didn't want to read too much into Diego's words, even if the image that jumped into his mind was that of Diego pounding away with quick repetitions, hips thrusting. Swallowing, the equine tried to refocus.

"Okay, that makes sense, was just curious. Hope I didn't interrupt."

"Not at all!" Diego pushed his forelock out of his eyes. "What brings you to Vegas if you're not enjoying yourself at the casinos, the shows, the dinners too?"

Pax grimaced, tucking his tail in close to his rump.

"I'm here with my family, it's supposed to be one last blowout…" He hesitated, combing his fingers through his mane. "But I'm not really into gambling. Not my scene at all."

"Seems daft to bring you then. And not much of a family vacation to me."

"Not really, but sometimes you have little say in these things."

"No?" Diego perched on the bench, looking up to Pax, eyes alight with genuine interest. "Why's that?"

Pax started to say something and stopped, searching for words. It was a fact – of course, he didn't have a choice with his parents. They were his parents and it would be ungrateful to not accept a holiday with them. It was expected of him.

"Well, I'll be working out what I want to do with my life soon, college finished two months ago and I'm just waiting on my results. I did miss a year in the middle though, I wasn't sure if I wanted to continue. They may not see me so much anymore when I move out, though who knows where I'm going. Supposed to be off to university, like my sister, but…"

Trailing off, Pax rolled his shoulders in a shrug.

"It doesn't matter. I'm sorry for going on. Just want to be out of there and away, you know? But how do you get somewhere when you don't know where you're going? Too much has happened already."

He rubbed the back of his hand across his muzzle, avoiding the stallion's eyes.

"I shouldn't be going on about this, I'm sorry."

"Hey." Diego rose and squeezed Pax's shoulder, fingers curling around. "It's okay. Sounds like you need a listening ear and someone to unload with. I can listen."

Twisting his body so that Diego's hand fell away, the stallion scratched his jaw. He'd only met Diego a short while ago – he couldn't say anything of his character or for his level of judgement. He was good in the gym though and knew his stuff, that much was strictly certain. The stallion observed Pax as he mulled over his thoughts, taking longer to reply than was polite.

"You don't like being touched so much, do you?"

Pax looked at Diego's hand, returning to his side, unaware that he had even pushed him away.

"Eh... I didn't mind that, not so much," he said, waving his own hand to reassure. "It's an automatic reaction now, didn't mean to shove you back."

"And why would you push someone away for putting their hand on your shoulder, unless you really didn't want them to touch you?" Diego softened, ears twitching. "It was me who overstepped there, you're supposed to maintain your boundaries, you know."

Diego took a half-step back and Pax held up his hands, shaking his head quickly to reassure.

"It's not that I don't want you touching me...I mean...wait. That came out wrong." His cheeks flushed with heat. "I just don't like *some* touching me. It's nothing against you. Not so much against guys either."

He sighed.

"Just, uh, girls, usually. They're way touchier than blokes."

"Why wouldn't you want a lady touching you? That's far from what I expected."

The palomino stallion folded his arms, muscles tightening and unconsciously making him appear larger and stronger than he was solely from his stature. Pax tapped his fingers on his bicep, drumming across his still damp coat.

"What did you expect?"

Diego smiled sheepishly.

"Maybe that you'd been beaten up at school?" He suggested. "I wasn't the most popular there either and got in a lot of fights. That's why I ended up at the gym, to make sure I won any fights that others started. Raw power did well enough to keep the idiots off my back, though I had to work harder at self-defence after they started ganging up on me. Was older by then. College, school done with."

He shrugged.

"As I said, not the most popular a few years ago. Doing much better now. It's a better place and a better time for me."

Pax's eyes widened. He would never have guessed that about the stallion who exuded the air that he had it all figured out, just like his sister. Only not in her arrogant manner. *Everything was in hand, thank you very much, move along, please.* Pax shook his head, looking at the stallion with renewed respect. He'd done right by himself, taken care of himself, despite his words ringing true of a hard time.

Diego scooped up his water bottle and took a long, deep swig of the clear liquid within. Without stopping his rough gulps, he sat and patted the bench beside him, taking his fill of water until Pax perched alongside, hesitant to seat himself comfortably. Shouldn't he be getting back to his routine or something? It felt wrong to use a gym bench as a conversational seat.

Wiping the back of his hand across his lips, Diego bumped Pax's shoulder with his, a light, fleeting contact that the equine didn't have time to move away from. It felt good to touch, sometimes, and he smiled. Diego put him at ease. That was what he needed.

"So, are you going to tell me what's going on in that head of yours, colt?"

He looked down at his hands, fingers curled around the edge of the bench. Did he dare? Was it wise? Diego had opened up to him. Pax rubbed his throat, taking his time to come up with the right answer, whatever that was. The only problem in the situation and life was that there was all too often no right answer. Like his choices in life ahead, university and so forth, he had no set path to follow. He may only gain guidance from sharing with another who could offer a guiding hand.

The stallion groaned inwardly. Why couldn't things ever be fucking simple?

Diego blinked, the one blue eye that Pax could see rounding large and kind. His fingertips grazed Pax's thigh through his jogging bottoms as he replaced his bottle on the floor. Where his fingers touched, Pax's nerves sparked with electric heat. The colt shuddered, yet did not shuffle away. What was this?

He shook himself. There was no time like the present to give something a try and, to be frank, where was the harm in speaking with Diego? If he laughed or said anything untoward, Pax did not have to see him again. Their contact could be fleeting, no strings attached. He took a deep breath, nostrils flaring as air rushed into his lungs.

"A long time ago, or at least it seems like an age ago, my sister, Sera, set me up with one of her friends."

The words spilled out, beyond Pax's control now that he had begun.

"It was nice. Nice at first. She was a mare, so of the same species, no issues raised there. Mom and dad liked her. They said we made a good couple. I was just turned eighteen, her twenty-one. Heh, I guess it wasn't all that long ago then."

He muddled up his words, though it did really feel like a long time since he'd been with Sera's friend. Listening silently, Diego rested his hand on Pax's shoulder, putting the weight of his hand down over several seconds. Pax trembled but appreciated the time allowed to become used to the sensation. It was reassuring, though the word did not encapsulate the true comfort it emanated.

"I was too young for it – maybe some stallions get it on when they're younger but, in hindsight…it wasn't right for me. Hindsight and all that. Looking ahead is tunnel vision. She wanted to have sex and, well, she did. Repeatedly."

Pax closed his eyes, the gym lights too bright through his shadowed eyelids.

"When I didn't want to anymore – couldn't even get it up sometimes, s'pose that speaks volumes – she got on top and made me do it, made me perform."

He hung his head, mane falling down the arch of his neck. There was not a sound in the gym besides their soft breathing, chests rising and falling out of unison.

"No one believes a bloke," Pax said, voice lowering to a whisper. "They think we want it all the time. I think I still said it was okay to her because she kept badgering me… But it's not *fucking* true. It would have been different, if it had been the other way round. Well, never would have happened, for a start. But no one thinks to defend a stallion against a mare. Maybe it would have been fine, if I'd been older, could have talked about it. Could have learned from it. But…no."

He was rambling. Like Sera – but in his own way too, hurt and confusion welling up from inside him. Diego's hand tightened on the stallion's shoulder. Without thinking, Pax covered Diego's hand with his own for a few seconds. He could not hold the touch, however, and moved away too soon, tail swishing as Diego leaned in closer, comforting Pax without words that would not convey what could never be said.

"So…that's the truth of it," he finished, splaying his hands flat on his thighs. "That's why I don't like others being clingy with me. Mostly comes out with femfurs, often mares, as they're cuddlier than guys. Usually. Always want to touch, touch and touch some more. Guys feel safer to me. If they push you too far, you're always open to retaliate. I feel like I know where I stand more."

Pax heaved a sigh.

"It's all rather stupid, I don't know what you must think of me. Shouldn't have ever let it happen, got in too deep and…I couldn't get out. Tried to tell my sister and she said I had to have been lying, told me off for screwing her friend as if she had never dragged me into it." The stallion grunted. "This all must sound fucking nuts."

"It makes sense," Diego said, quick to reassure and slide his hand around to the stallion's opposite shoulder for a one-armed hug that he released Pax from before he had the opportunity to feel uncomfortable. "I'm very sorry that happened to you. Some furs don't understand the effect they have, the influence, constantly chasing their own, selfish needs. It's the way of it, but that doesn't mean we have to sit here and like it. Sadly, there's not many words that can help."

He licked his lips, finding the desired words.

"Only, I will say that you didn't deserve this, not one bit. It wasn't your fault, Pax. I hope you can understand that one day."

They sat there in companionable silence, Pax rubbing circles into the back of his own hand. It had been good to finally say everything aloud without being interrupted by eye rolls. The words had been not many, yet their meaning appreciated. Pax exhaled, releasing a breath that he had not realised he had been holding. Was it really not his fault? That was a question for another day. For now, it was a relief to have everything in the open and, temporarily, out of his head. It had been there for too long and Diego… He'd listened. He had not pushed. He was just there, helping.

Diego clapped, the sharp sound startling the stallion whose ears flattened to his skull. The stallion dropped him a wink and a knowing smile that told more than his actions.

Trust me.

"Come on!"

Diego offered his hand and Pax took it after a moment's hesitation, allowing Diego to pull him up to his hooves.

"You may not have had the best few years since then, but life is what you make of it. You're in the gym, so I'll call this therapy of a different ilk. Just like *Lucky Sevens. Diego* therapy!"

Though his tone was jokey, the stallion's eyes rang serious.

"Get in the half-rack, move the bench. We're doing squats."

Wordlessly, Pax complied, scooting out the bench that he'd used earlier – had so much been said in such a short span of time? – and set the hooks for the barbell so that the bar would cross below his collarbone. Set up ready for Diego, the stallion glanced back, tail swishing curiously. Just what did the horse have in mind? Squats certainly had not been what he was expecting after spilling his life story, or at least a notable part, but the stallion seemed to have something in mind. He was full of surprises, it had to be said. Diego nodded encouragingly, eyes bright.

"Go on, load up your working weight."

Pax loaded the plates on the bar to a respectable weight and attached the clamps to keep them from sliding off. Not waiting for further instruction, he popped his head under the barbell and put it across his back on his traps, only then looking back with a little trepidation.

Diego took up position behind Pax in the place of a traditional spotter who would support the weight and assist with the trainee's form as and when required. Though he shuddered at having the warmth of the stallion so close, Pax gulped and stared at the wall, resolution hardening. Diego huffed warm breath over the back of his neck, edging closer.

"Go on, start your set and work to your best reps," Diego said. "Don't mind me – I won't touch unless you're about to drop the weight. Safety pins are in place, don't worry."

Breathing deeply and evenly, Pax set the bar more comfortably on his traps and took a step back, allowing the weight to settle. Diego moved with him, ensuring that he did not get in the way, and nickered encouragingly. He sunk into his first squat, back flat and rump pushing out, grunting with the effort it took to rise even that first time. It was too fucking heavy! He'd overestimated what he would be able to do – yet again.

He shook his head, mumbling that he couldn't squat the weight and moved to put the bar back on the hooks, intending to reduce the number of plates on the bar. But Diego wasn't having any of that. Diego held him in position, supporting the bar so that he did not topple his charge off balance with the force applied.

"Nope – it's not that easy to give up with me. Keep going. One more. Again."

Pax ground his teeth until his jaw ached, exhaling sharply as pain ripped through his muscles. He couldn't do it – it was too heavy! How was any horse supposed to lift that? The bar tilted and Diego nudged it back into position with his fingertips as Pax sank into a low squat and, somehow, stood with the weight. The bar bent very slightly, bowing across his back, and Pax grunted, renewed determination rekindling in his chest.

Diego huffed against his mane, close, hands assisting with the lightest of guiding touches wherever they were needed. He only had to keep the colt squatting.

"Every time you stand up with the weight on your shoulders, you're letting what happened know it can't beat you, it can't best you," Diego growled in Pax's ear, fingertips brushing the bar as he faltered on his last clean rep but not taking the weight away. "This is *you* smashing through and coming out stronger the other side. Not everything happens for a reason, but you can learn from it! Pushing iron can clear your head, so you can think… So, make that bar *move!*"

And, just like that, the bar rose for an eighth repetition, three more reps than Pax had ever managed at that weight working solo. He pushed the bar back on to the hooks and whinnied, the sound shrill and proud as his tail flagged, reminding him of a different kind of high. It was only one set, one to begin with, but it was a start, a beginning. Rolling his shoulders, Pax looked down at his hands, palms stinging. Something slipped from his shoulders with that lift and it was not the bar. He had not failed. He had *won*.

Or would win, one step and one day at a time. He was not so coltish as to think all behind him already. Trauma took longer than that, but Pax hadn't had the chance to even try to heal when it had all been kept inside. Yet his hooves were now on solid ground. Behind him, chest brushing Pax's straightened back, Diego nickered and clapped his shoulder, congratulating him with a rough little shake that Pax could not help but laugh breathlessly at.

"Thanks..." Pax panted, tongue thick in his mouth as he dragged air into his lungs. "That helped. I think."

"You're more than welcome, colt." Diego lipped his mane affectionately. "But it's not a one-off cure. This is only to show you that you can achieve whatever you put your mind to. You only have to put in the time and work. Some help doesn't go amiss either, if you can find a stallion as delightful as yours truly."

Pax chuckled, glancing at the stallion as the male moved in a sudden burst of motion, angling his body away. Pax's ears twitched and he half-turned to follow him. Why was he holding himself in such an awkward position, back hunched as if to hide? Was the equine...blushing? Pax shook his head. It had to be a trick of the light. Diego wouldn't blush. How silly to think such a thing.

Diego shifted uncomfortably, but there was one thing that a stallion could never conceal. Though it took him several agonisingly long moments to come to his senses, Pax's eyes dropped to the obvious bulge in the equine's jogging bottoms, tenting out the front as a half-hard shaft proudly dropped. Pax's jaw fell slack as Diego whickered, hiding his searing muzzle. Pax *stared*.

It caught him off-guard, a burning flash of heat that made his tail swish, sheath plumping out with a cock that had not been touched in far, far too long. Desire that he had not felt since he was a much younger horse – too young for deeds done – flared through his veins like wildfire, potent in its intoxication. As the black stallion held up his hands and backed away, embarrassed, Pax crept closer, ducking under the barbell with his eyes firmly fixed on the stallion's bulge.

It was crazy. He should have left. He should have laughed it off with Diego as a mishap at the gym, pulled the stallion back to a safe, level playing field with him. And then he didn't.

"Ah, I'm sorry…" Diego rubbed his muzzle. "I know I was helping you and all, but you just put yourself in such position there… Can't help but notice your physique, colt. I'm not a pervert, I swear!"

Standing nose to nose, Pax pressed his lips to those of the stallion's, lifting his arms around the horse's neck even as Diego jerked back in shock. Pax's lips parted, tongue questing for a new experience as he moved too quickly to consider the insanity of what he was doing, the stranger whose bulge ground against his own. Their tongues danced together and Pax groaned into the kiss, pressing close as Diego's fingers stroked through his mane. He had lifted the weight. He could do anything.

So, Pax sank into the kiss, his heart lifting the moment Diego responded to him. He hadn't realised just how erotic that could be, that throb and pulse of knowing someone else was as into him as he was into them. How could that even be so? He didn't know enough about attraction to say, but it all seemed like fate that Diego and he came to be there at that exact time, their bodies aching with a familiar heat.

He had to be close to him as Diego's fingers softly combed through his mane, separating out the strands of hair from their neighbours. Even though there were no nerve endings directly at the base of each strand, it sent a shiver through his body simply from that subtle manipulation alone.

How could someone be so tender with him? Sure, Pax was young and he knew things were happening very quickly, but he didn't want to stop. It was too good, leaning into the kiss, his tongue dipping just a little deeper into Diego's mouth.

Pax had kissed before, though not much. He hadn't done too much, experimenting a little and fumbling his way through earlier encounters. It wasn't that he hadn't wanted to – things just hadn't seemed to line up so he could take the chances offered to him. If he liked someone, they didn't like him. And if someone liked him, he'd been told about it a couple of times far after the fact – when it was too late to do anything about it.

It was clumsy and awkward…but he was still young. An adult, yes, but still learning and still growing. It was not so bad to have someone to share things with, someone who had a little more experience, who could more gently show him the way.

Diego's lips shifted against his and the horse's hand rested on his chest gently, his fingers splaying out. Pax shuddered bodily, a ripple going through him.

Breaking the kiss and sharing breath, Diego's eyes shone. The older stallion stayed close to him, barely moving away, his nostrils puckering and flaring as he breathed a little more heavily. Pax would have smirked to see that he'd had an effect on Diego too, though his head was still pleasantly spinning.

"No one has to know we're here," Diego whispered with bated breath, curling his fingers into Pax's mane. "The door's locked…or will be locked. With the key on this side, of course!"

He chuckled, eyes dropping longingly to Pax's crotch, bulge tenting out. Pax wriggled and tried to back away, just to put a little space there, but that only made his rising hard-on all the more obvious.

Yet stallions weren't known for being discreet with their passions and Pax didn't need to hide. Stepping back only drew Diego's eyes down. Pax tried to cover his crotch with his hands, but there was really not all that much he could do.

Diego nickered softly, raising his hand to brush Pax's cheek with the back of his fingers. The stallion shivered, relaxing ever so slightly.

"I wouldn't lock you in with no way out."

Pax quivered. In his mind's eye, he saw the black equine moving over him, cock hard and kissing the length of his own. What would that feel like? How big even was Diego?

The stallion drew him in, gently, and he let Diego hug him, his big hands sweeping down Pax's back. Yet his mind was elsewhere, focused on how hard and muscular the stallion's chest was against his, how he felt like he could simply melt into it, forgetting where he was and everything that had been holding him back so far.

"You're so sweet… But this is all your choice," Diego said, sure to make himself quite clear. "No one is going to make you do anything, I just had to say something. Kind of just came out like that. You know?"

Pax gasped, his chin on Diego's shoulder as a shiver rant through his whole body. Why did it feel right with a stallion? That may have been why things just hadn't worked out before with others. He'd only tried being with femfurs, although it just hadn't gone smoothly. There was not an ounce of worry from his times with ladies that had no interest in him as a stallion or his pleasure, his love or his life, remained, despite the fretting tremble of his upper lip. The slight worry of wanting to do well with Diego felt clean, untainted: the butterflies in his stomach before a storm that he wished to ride out to the very end.

Maybe he was gay. Maybe he was bisexual. That was for Pax to decide, whenever the time suited him.

The stallion made his decision, gently, in the back of his mind. His active mind, conscious thought, would have to be clear about things very shortly, but there was enough time for that.

Diego nuzzled into his neck and Pax's breath caught. Fast, too fast. But in a good way. He nickered, though could not make himself step away from the stallion's muscled warmth. Worry was one thing – he wanted this. And badly too.

It was worth it. It would all be worth it, easing by that worry with someone holding his hand the whole time.

"You don't have to do anything you don't want to do, colt."

Diego exhaled slowly, warm breath wafting over Pax's neck, muscle twitching wherever the horse's hands roamed. Repeating that was important to Pax and the stallion's ears twitched as he caught on to it, paying close attention to everything Diego said. It was as if his senses had been heightened, though his body focused intently on the feel of the stallion against him.

Could another body really burn like that? He licked his lips lightly, arching his neck as Diego nipped and nibbled, very lightly, at his neck. The stallion's teeth followed the line of muscle in it as Pax's lips parted in a faint smile.

"We can leave right now, or even just finish our workout, if that's what you want to do. This is in your control."

The palomino snorted, shaking his mane off his neck. Every fibre of his being sang to the stallion's touch, experience thrumming through his fingertips as they grazed down Pax's side to his hips and buttocks. He wanted it. Yet, he wavered.

"I don't know if I can do this…" Pax admitted at last, head rolling back as the stallion lipped at his throat, nipping the line of his jaw. "It's not that I've…ah…never had sex before…not with… Fuck, you already know that. But I've never been with a guy… I don't know what to do."

"I can teach you, colt, if that is what you want. But there's always time."

The stallion dropped a kiss on Pax's nose, fingers curling in to squeeze his rump, a cheeky edge to the cocky tilt of his head. Squeaking, Pax unwittingly pushed his backside into Diego's hands and the stallion smirked, tugging Pax's jogging bottoms down to his thighs. The equine whinnied as his cock sprung out, having not worn any underwear to the gym, a grey and pink mottled shaft bobbing proudly once released from the restraining fabric.

Diego murmured his appreciation and licked his lips with a very pink tongue, easing to his knees. Pax stood stock still, not knowing what to do, though he still gave Diego a shaky, clear nod of permission. That was okay. He could do that, even though heat rushed to his cheeks and crawled down his neck at having his cock exposed in the blink of an eye.

The stallion curled his fingers around his shaft on the underside, weighting Pax's cock in his hand. He licked his lips obviously and Pax's eyes hungrily tracked every little movement of his. His peripheral vision caught the twitches of his body, yet he was more focused on the slide of the stallion's hand along his length. It bumped over the medial ring and teased further down, some of the skin pulling along with Diego's hand where there was a little more friction.

"Ah… Oh…" Pax moaned, ears twitching all over the place, not knowing which direction to face. "That feels…really nice."

"Not too exposed?" Diego said, checking in with him, even though the older stallion had been the one to push things further. "You're so big already."

The rest of Pax's cock, where it had still been ever so slightly soft, fleshed out a little more, coming up to fully hard. Diego thumbed the horse's shaft and played with the medial ring, his fingers lightly indenting Pax's flesh, though he always released the pressure. It was hardly an unpleasant kind of pleasure, however, and the stallion nickered, his lips wobbling lightly as his muzzle twitched. It had been a while indeed since someone had touched his cock quite like that.

"Oh, very nice, colt..." He checked in and brushed his lips over the head of Pax's cock, touch velvety. "I'm going to make you feel very, very good. Just relax now, my colt."

Taking Pax's cock in one hand, he wrapped his fingers more securely around the girth, not quite managing to make his finger and thumb meet around. Size didn't matter, however, although Diego was larger than Pax. Pax nickered and stomped, a hoof coming down harder on the floor, the thick matting, though it didn't make much noise.

The stallion wasted no time, leaning in to lap over the head, tasting pre cum and the sweet aroma of stallion musk that embodied taste and scent simultaneously. His cock throbbed, lust rising, and he parted his lips wide to take the head of Pax's cock into his muzzle, sliding down until the head kissed the back of his throat. Pax trembled, his quads tightening, yet he had to lock his legs to stay upright.

Pax moaned as Diego's tongue squeezed to the underside of his shaft, rubbing and slathering the fat shaft in saliva that would be sorely needed. There was not exactly any lubrication to be had there, for they were in the gym and not tucked away in one of their bedrooms. Diego gulped around the cock in his mouth, a gleam of drool at the corner of his lips. Against himself, his eyes narrowed, cock straining against the fabric of his gym trousers. A stallion had needs as strong as a colt, though it was Pax who was important there, taking all Diego's attention.

Shifting from hoof to hoof, Pax's hands wandered, finding no place to rest until finding Diego's head and winding lightly into his mane. It felt right, yet he didn't want to appear as if he was pushing Diego's head down either. It was just so alluring, greedily drinking it all in as his worry quieted, bit by bit.

His tail swished mindlessly, eyes on the show as inch after inch of his cock disappeared into a hot, willing muzzle, which was all too eager to please. He'd never known that a blowjob was meant to feel so good. His hips bucked of their own accord, thrusting his deeper and nudging his shaft down the stallion's throat. He worried for half a second that he was making Diego uncomfortable before remembering that equines lacked a gag reflex: he'd seen it in practice.

"Ah…" Pax trembled as the stallion's lips slid nearly to the very base of his cock, tightly pursed around his length. "Aren't you going to show me…too? Pull your trousers down? You were the one getting hard, after all…"

Pax blushed, wiggling in place. How did he put it? He didn't want Diego to miss out on his own pleasure too, just because he was focusing all of his attention on Pax. That wasn't right.

"You want me as much as I want you."

He trailed off with a feeble chuckle. Diego did not pull his muzzle from Pax's cock but obliged by yanking his trousers down to his knees along with his boxer shorts to reveal a dropped pink shaft with the faintest splash of black mottling. Pax's heart leapt into his throat, cock pulsing with a spurt of pre-cum that Diego gulped down, throat working around his shaft. Grunting, Diego bobbed his muzzle and took the full length down his throat, only then coming up for a quick intake of air through his nostrils, eyes lidded from pleasure. The palomino twisted his fingers more roughly into Diego's mane and bucked, tail flicking as his buttocks clenched.

Oh, that felt good, really good. The hard length of Diego's pink shaft throbbed obviously and it was all Pax could do to crane his neck and keep his eyes on it. He simply couldn't drag them away, moaning aloud, his hips bucking as he haphazardly speared his cock down Diego's throat. His thrusts were rough and unfeeling, yet he knew what he wanted and Diego encouraged him on with throaty, muffled nickers, so he was still well within the realm of their boundaries.

As Pax thrust, Diego's tongue curled against the underside of his smooth cock, playing around the head every time he drew back far enough. Yet Diego didn't draw back all the way, not allowing Pax's cock to spring free of his lips at any time. Any pre-cum drooled straight on to the stallion's tongue or down his throat as he took Pax deep, his throat shifting as he swallowed around the thick length of stallion meat.

So close! Pax jerked as the familiar rush of erotic delight tickled his senses with increasing persistence. He rolled his head from one shoulder to the other, eyes closed against the glare of unflattering overhead lights. His buttocks clenched and he tried to think of anything that may stave off the oncoming storm. His cock throbbed and Diego suckled harder as if sensing his predicament. Pax shook his head, upper lip curling back as he sifted through the scent of musky stallion, heady in the air. It was all too much, much too much. No… He had to hold out. Just a little longer. He could do it. He just wanted to enjoy a little longer.

Taking note of his sudden stillness, Diego withdrew, the flat head of Pax's cock finally popping from his lips and drooping under its own weight. Though he grumbled at the decrease in sensation, balanced on the brink of an explosive orgasm, he was relieved for the respite, calming with a tremble that ran the length of his body from his nose to his fetlocks.

Diego flashed him a brilliant grin and dived to the side, reclaiming his own gym bag from where he had dropped it beside the half-rack. Pax blinked. It seemed like a very long time ago that he had been in the rack with Diego spotting him, driving him on to achieve his goals and shift the weight of the bar and all that held him back. The stallion nickered.

"Quick, colt." Diego blew him a kiss, tossing him a small, capped tube from the red bag that Pax barely reacted in time to catch. "I didn't lock the door or anything like I said I would, anyone could walk in. I know it's late and…fuck, I want you. I want you so bad, colt. Please?"

Pax wondered if Diego really even had to ask permission. Privacy seemed like a foreign concept with his cock swaying like a flagpole caught by a too strong wind. It was kind of cute to see the stronger, larger stallion on his knees begging too. It made him feel stronger.

With everything that had happened, Pax was the one who called the shots. He was the one in control.

And that was a very nice feeling indeed.

Pax smirked, lips quirking up almost unwillingly. Cock throbbing, it twitched as blood pulsed through the length and denied a supply to more thoughtful organs that may have had better use for it. Feeling shy was out the window. It was a good thing that he had a guide to reassure him that his judgement was spot on; risks could be fun too. Glancing down at the bottle clasped between his hands, Pax raised an eyebrow.

"Moisturiser?" Pax chuckled and turned it over in his hands. "You sure that's going to be enough? We'd need more, right? You're kind of... Well, you're...big."

"Not for me, colt," Diego winked. "I know this one, heh, doesn't make anything sore, even if you shouldn't really use it as lube often. Dunno what would happen then. Here."

Resting his elbows on the black, padded bench, Diego rocked his rump up and wriggled his buttocks teasingly, tail flagged high to show off his tight pucker, clenching down on nothing. Pax swallowed, approaching with his cock in one hand and the moisturiser in the other, feeling as if his mind was no longer connected with his body. It was as if he had fallen into the most wonderful of dreams, though everything was certainly real.

Licking his lips nervously, Pax squeezed a generous dose of creamy white moisturiser on to his cock and spread it along the whole length, adding more so that it did not simply soak into his mottled grey and pink skin. It felt nice, at least, though he would have much preferred to have the stallion's mouth wrapped hotly around his cock, or even his hand.

"And...you'll be okay?"

Pax bit his tongue, eyes wide. He had to ask, for the stallion looked so sweet, laid out before him with his tail hiked in display. If he'd had less care and concern for the black horse, he would have mounted him right there and then, fumbled and thrust in with a stallion scream that would have alerted the entire hotel to their tryst. Peering back, Diego shot him a reassuring grin, ears swivelling to pay him every ounce of attention he had to give.

"Trust me, colt. I'll be just fine. Better than fine."

That would have to be reassurance enough for the golden stud. Pax rubbed his cock and stepped up to the stallion, letting his shaft drop on to Diego's muscled buttocks. By the gods, they were perfect, swelling with years of building muscle and definition. Diego grunted as the flat cock-tip slipped between his cheeks, the stallion grinding it back and forth with a moan.

"Fuck me, colt…"

Pax had no strength with which to resist, pushing Diego's tail up with the backs of his fingers. The head of his cock pulsed, as if the flare was going to swell all the way right there and then, although Pax wanted to enjoy every moment. He didn't want to rush it, even if there was still a risk to be had in using the gym for such activities.

He was no fool but as they said: when in Vegas…

The stallion grinned, running his hand over the equine's buttocks, admiring the tight pull of muscle beneath his black hide. Diego snorted and flagged his tail for him, allowing Pax to dig his fingers in. There wasn't much fat in the slightest for him to indent his fingers into, the muscle harder and much less yielding.

"Oh, damn…"

Holding his breath, Pax rubbed the well-lubricated tip of his cock over the horse's tail hole before daring to push in and bore down with the gentleness of a long-time lover. For a moment, it seemed as if the stallion was trying to keep him out, pushing against the head, and then half the length of Pax's cock slipped in with hardly any resistance, stretching out the stallion's tail hole. He groaned, panting heavily, and arched his back, rocking into Pax's first steady thrust, which ground in deep until the stallion's crotch was flush with his rump.

The black stallion grunted and flipped his tail higher, swatting Pax across the chest as he struggled to contain the pleasure wracking his body. Screwing up his muzzle, Pax pushed his chest out, his own vest top askew. He could have spent himself in a matter of seconds, but he wanted Diego to feel as good as he did. The stallion deserved every second of pleasure Pax could deliver and more.

Pax experimented slightly, rolling his hips with long, fluid strokes – as deep as he felt he could go. More of his tail pushed inside, gently stretching out Diego's tail hole, but it seemed their makeshift lube was doing its job. Pax had heard somewhere that lube wasn't always needed for backdoor play if those doing it went slowly. It seemed like a good thing to employ even then.

So, he breathed in slowly and evenly, despite the judder in his chest. He pressed his fingers into the stallion's rump as if he was trying to pull his rear cheeks apart, just so he could enjoy the sight of every inch of his own cock being swallowed up by Diego's ass. The stallion was tight, wonderfully so, though the friction was not enough to stop him from grinding back and forth.

Even pulling back felt like it was too much as Pax grunted and stomped, swishing his tail as tension mounted. Of course, it was the good kind of tension, his hide darkening in patches as he sweated, heat rising. Yet it was Diego who stole the show under him, licking his lips and snorting heavily, rolling his hips back to tease a little more of Pax's cock into him. The medial ring popped in and Pax gulped hard as he was forced to drag it back out, only to thrust again. Even that action was a manner of delicious torture.

"Ah…fuck, colt…" Diego whinnied, head lowered to brush his nose over the bench. "You're thick…ah…"

"Is it too much? I can pull out if you want. I don't want to hurt you."

Pax didn't want to pull out but would if Diego needed him to, of course. Diego, however, shook his head, mane falling to the left side of his neck.

"No, colt… Fuck me. Good and deep."

With his hands on Diego's hips, Pax took him at his word and thrust, learning the first nuances of male pleasure with a light-headed moan. His cock disappeared again and again into the stallion's rump, each thrust feeling as if it was the very first all over again. Would that this was his first time! It would have been a far better first time and experience for him, finally coming together with another as he was meant to.

Pax rolled his shoulders backwards, fingers groping the fine stallion's ass. How did anyone bear such sensation? A hot, clenching hole around his rod, dragging him in more with every thrust? And, below the stallion's belly hung an equally delicious pole of flesh, drooling pre cum in a pool down to the floor. The cleaners would have fun the next morning, he had no doubt about that. Gasping, Pax drove in harder and deeper, just as Diego asked, glutes clenching to add more power to his thrusts.

The rhythm came naturally to him, the more that he thrust, as if he had been born to do it. Having the stallion beneath him was inherently right. Though he wondered one thing as Diego moaned and arched back, whinnying for more.

What would that cock feel like under *his* tail?

Rutting, the stallion's nickered and ground together, Pax's hips slapping into Diego's rump with every thrust. Their whinnies rose, blending together into one, as sweat beaded on Pax's coat. Diego didn't seem to notice droplets landing on his back, splattering his t-shirt, head ducked down over the other side of the bench as he pushed his hips up as far towards Pax as was physically possible in the position. He splayed his legs apart for balance, grunting every time Pax thrust in, the palomino getting into the act and pounding his tail hole with enough force to send a throb of soreness through his rear.

It would all be worth it, for those moments alone.

Pax closed his eyes against the gym lights, obnoxiously glancing off Diego's coat, and tucked his chin down to his chest. It was unlike anything he had ever felt before, to have a stallion bucking beneath him, eager for every inch he had to give. And, with so much pleasure, came the roar of an unstoppable force that not even the best of intentions could hold back behind the floodgates for more than a few heartbeats. Gripping Diego's tail, Pax neighed and hammered in, hips driving in short, unforgiving thrusts that made the stallion quake.

Time seemed to draw out, moment by moment, allowing him to sink into just how every thrust felt. The stallion's rump pulled around him, as if Diego was trying to pull his cream from him, yet that was just Pax's mind trying to make sense of everything happening in the moment. He was not experienced and his mind tried to cling on to anything familiar to him, even as his stomach ached and something deeper, lower down, clenched crudely.

His hand tried to drop, seeking Diego's cock, yet it was all about them in the moment, the heady slap of Pax's hips slamming into the horse's rump, over and over again. Diego grunted, neck arching, and Pax could not look away from the beauty of him, how the stallion held it all so casually that it was as if it was all purely natural to him.

Yet Pax was young and Diego hit every last one of his needs, every spot he could have possibly needed stroked. There was no way he could hold back, not as his eyelids fluttered, struggling to see.

This is it.

It was too late for Pax to hold back from climax for a single moment more – needs overcame desire and he snapped his eyes open, nostrils sharply flared for a last intake of breath before his world lost focus. He slammed in, losing himself in the moment, and ejaculated with a stallion scream of release, falling over the larger horse and letting the equine support his entire weight as his cock throbbed, filling his tail hole with thick spurts of cum.

Pulsing more and more until Pax feared orgasm would drain him dry, steal every last drop from his sore balls, he thrust weakly until cum drooled from the stallion's ring, forced out along his length. The creamy offering marked the edge of his sheath, though neither would concern themselves with the mess, not even as it dripped down the back of Diego's legs and stuck into his dark tail.

Diego was not to go forgotten, however, and Pax wearily lipped at the base of his neck, reaching around the stallion's cut abdomen – his hand brushing the stallion's abs – to stroke his cock with quick, untrained pumps. The stallion grunted, flagged his tail and arched against him, head shooting up to press his cheek to Pax's as the head of his cock flared dramatically, pre cum leaking in a steady stream in prelude to climax. Rocking his head to the side, Diego gave a gasp that shuddered through him as he reached orgasm, swift to cum as a cock softened under his tail. His whole body trembled as his balls tightened up to his body, just that fraction, and he dropped his chest completely to the bench with Pax on top of him, cock shooting cum to paint the floor for an impressive distance as pleasure ripped any remaining notion of hiding their liaison in the gym from his mind.

Struggling to turn his head far enough around, cock still spurting, Diego nuzzled Pax, sharing a brief kiss before he had to hang his muzzle low once more. Breath came with difficulty and Pax pulled his hands to the bench, taking some of the weight off his partner as his tail waved high, covering Diego's shoulders in kisses and nips even as his arms trembled.

"Mmmph, you really are something special, colt…"

Pax pressed his muzzle into the back of Diego's neck, for the first time in his young life, completely and utterly content. He only wished that the night did not have to end. And it didn't, if not for a little while. For a time, they had each other and could recover in each other's arms. If Pax was lucky, perhaps there would even be a round two. A colt could dream.

He held the stallion tighter, hiding the single tear squeezing from the corner of his eye.

Thank you.

Words were needed and words were most certainly useful, yet the stallions had to move quickly there. They kissed and twisted their necks around, so their lips met as Pax drew his cock from Diego's ass. The head popped free, even as his cock softened, and they gasped.

That night, Diego did something more for Pax than either of them could ever have anticipated, but only time would tell just how things would change. Whether or not they would come together again was an open-ended question and one that the light of day would have to tell the tale of. Some things could be sweetened by a late hour and others required thought and clarity.

Together, they cleaned up, kissed and went their separate ways that night, although the touches of the stallions lingered. It was as if they didn't really want to separate, sharing a look from the other end of the corridor as Pax made to head back to his shared room for the night.

Vegas had given him more than Pax had ever anticipated could be found there. And it was not typical, by any means.

*

Packing his bags in the hotel room the next morning, Pax's mind wandered from his sister's constant chatter of the night before, much too late for him to take in comprehensibly. She said he had missed so much out at the roulette tables and slot machines but, in all honesty, he couldn't see what he had missed at all. More than ever before, he felt secure in who he was and he knew where he wanted to go and what he wanted to do with his life. He would attend university. He would do a joint honours degree, a little safety net in the sciences with options open to him. He had a life ahead of him and renewed certainty in who he was. It didn't matter what anyone else thought. He knew that now. But lessons had to be learned for oneself.

In his holdall bag was a business card with a certain horse's phone number scrawled across the back in scratchy pen, the ink half-dying. During the early neon hours of the morning, while Sera snored off her drink, he had cast his eyes over and over that number, unable to fathom just how he had been lucky enough to acquire it. He had not even seen the stallion slip it into the pocket of his jogging bottoms as they left the gym, a wily trickster indeed while Pax had been too shy to ask for it when they shared a goodbye kiss that had turned into lust, dragging one another back to Pax's room. Though it was more than impressive, in his eyes, that an equine of Diego's size had been able to slip anything into him at all.

Pax's lips twisted as he blushed at the memories, the hot stallion pressing him down into the bed, rushed and clumsy in fear of his sister returning, hours after they had left the gym. But there was more to their liaison than sex alone, a kindling of hope that Pax held close to his heart.

Looking out the window to the bright sunshine, Pax smiled and hauled the bag up on to his shoulder, heavy with belongings snuck into the holdall by his sister. She wasn't so bad after all. Sera hadn't meant any harm, though she refused to account for any harm. He would only have to be strong enough to work through it, with a side of help. His new friend had taught him that. And perhaps his family would accept him regardless of their inclinations towards mares who loved cats and stallions who loved stallions. They loved him – he knew that. He would not know unless he tried, unless he took that leap into the unknown and tackled the aftermath in his stride. The stallion would be prepared for everything and anything.

Although he would not tell his family of Diego for many more years to come, the Spanish stallion and how he stole his heart, cliché even in his warm, brown eyes, there were many more good things in life to come, experience and days to make him feel alive. The furs walking through life with him were what made it life and he shuddered at the memory of Diego's arms wrapped around him, holding him protectively close as he trembled. He yearned to feel those arms tight around him again, muscle flexing. Diego could protect him as he could look after the stallion too. Yes, experiences were the fuel of life itself. It was those very experiences, risks and love giggled over in the dawn, that made life worth living. He could not have learned that at a better time. A few days later and it could have all been too late for a life cast away and locked in disarray.

He was a lucky "colt" indeed.

His smile too wide to contain, Pax opened the hotel room door and stepped out to greet the rest of his life, phone clutched in his hand to dial a number that he had already memorised. Holding his breath, he trotted down the corridor, ignoring the looks from the hotel cleaner as he bounded over her red plastic caddy of supplies, a duster clutched in the older husky's gloved hand. It didn't matter what looks he got when all his attention was on the phone ringing, Pax's heart pounding like a runaway horse, torn loose from the traces of harness.

The phone stopped ringing and the stallion exhaled a breath he had not known he had been holding, slowing to a much-needed halt outside the lift. A familiar stallion nickered to him through the phone.

"Hey."

Not everything that happened in Vegas needed to stay in Vegas.

For Pax and Diego, their time together was just getting started.

Thank you for reading and I hope that everything was very much enjoyed!

Ready for more? Check out my author website for more furry fiction and where you can purchase my books!

https://linktr.ee/amethystmare

Cover art illustrated by Kai_art; they are contactable via e-mail for work enquiries.

dongvieck10@gmail.com